EDDIE *and his Big Deals*

By the Same Author

EDDIE THE DOG HOLDER. 1966
ROBERT ROWS THE RIVER. 1965
EDDIE'S GREEN THUMB. 1964
HERE COMES THE BUS! 1963
SNOWBOUND WITH BETSY. 1962
ANNIE PAT AND EDDIE. 1960
EDDIE AND LOUELLA. 1959
BETSY'S WINTERHOUSE. 1958
EDDIE MAKES MUSIC. 1957
BETSY'S BUSY SUMMER. 1956
EDDIE AND HIS BIG DEALS. 1955
BETSY AND THE CIRCUS. 1954
EDDIE'S PAY DIRT. 1953
THE MIXED-UP TWINS. 1952
EDDIE AND GARDENIA. 1951
BETSY'S LITTLE STAR. 1950
EDDIE AND THE FIRE ENGINE. 1949
PENNY GOES TO CAMP. 1948
LITTLE EDDIE. 1947
Published by William Morrow & Company

PENNY AND PETER. 1946
BETSY AND THE BOYS. 1945
HERE'S A PENNY. 1944
BACK TO SCHOOL WITH BETSY. 1943
PRIMROSE DAY. 1942
BETSY AND BILLY. 1941
TWO AND TWO ARE FOUR. 1940
"B" IS FOR BETSY. 1939
Published by Harcourt, Brace & World

EDDIE

and his Big Deals

Written and Illustrated by
CAROLYN HAYWOOD

WILLIAM MORROW AND COMPANY
New York   *1955*

Chapter I of this book, "A New Neighbor for Eddie," appeared in the
June, 1955, issue of *Jack and Jill* magazine. Copyright 1955 by the Curtis
Publishing Company.

Eleventh Printing, November, 1969

To

EDITH EMERSON

this book is lovingly dedicated

CONTENTS

ACKNOWLEDGMENT

The author wishes to express her gratitude to Mary Hornby Lea of San Angelo, Texas, her Peacock Consultant.

EDDIE *and his Big Deals*

CHAPTER 1

A NEW NEIGHBOR FOR EDDIE

I T WAS Saturday morning. Eddie Wilson was raking
up the leaves on the front lawn when a big moving
van drew up and stopped in front of the house next
door. The house had been empty for several months,
but recently the *For Sale* sign on the front lawn had
been removed, so the Wilsons knew that they would
soon have new neighbors.

Eddie and his brothers, Rudy, Joe, and Frank, hoped that the new family would include some boys. "We need some more fellows for our football team," Rudy, the eldest of the Wilson boys, had said. Joe and Frank, the twins, heartily agreed.

"Well, I hope they don't have any girls," Eddie said. "Girls are a nuisance. They're poison."

"Eddie!" his mother exclaimed. "What a terrible thing to say, when you know so many nice little girls. Think of Anna Patricia."

"Poison!" said Eddie. "They're all poison."

Now the new family was arriving. At least, their furniture was arriving. Eddie threw down his rake and ran to the stone wall that separated the two driveways. It was a fine seat from which to watch the unloading of the moving van.

He watched the driver turn and back the van into the driveway. He saw the men get out and take down the chain that held the door in the back of the van tightly closed. It fell away with a clanging rattle. The bolts were unfastened and the doors swung open. The van was bulging with furniture.

Eddie loved nothing better than watching an unloading. Anything and everything that came out of vans interested Eddie. There was always the chance that something might be thrown away which would turn out to be valuable property. Eddie's family would call it junk, but that did not make any difference to Eddie. There had been times when even his father had been forced to admit that Eddie had brought home "some swell stuff."

Now the moving men were beginning to unpack the van. They were taking out long rolls of carpets and rugs.

In a few minutes a station wagon drove up behind the truck and stopped. It sounded like a dogcatcher's wagon, it was so full of barking dogs. It was packed to the roof, and sticking out on all sides, like the bristles of a porcupine, were broom handles, mop handles, brush handles, shovel handles, the vacuum-cleaner handle, and the lawn-mower handle.

Eddie saw a woman get out of the driver's seat. She pulled three gray poodles out after her and ran across the lawn and up to the front door of the house. She put the key in the lock, opened the door wide, and went inside.

Eddie went over to the station wagon to get a better look. It was bulging with just the kind of things Eddie liked to look at. As he reached the side of the car, a voice from inside said, "Hey, open the door, will you?"

Eddie was surprised, for he hadn't seen anyone, but he opened the door and a whole pile of hatboxes began to move and then to topple over. Suddenly Eddie found himself in the midst of a shower of hatboxes. Then, out from behind the boxes, came a head tied up in a white bandage. Above the bandage Eddie could see some bright red hair. It seemed like a crew cut. As more of the owner of the head emerged, Eddie could see a plaid shirt. Then two legs in blue jeans wriggled out. Eddie was delighted. Here was a new friend about his own age.

"I'm Sidney Stewart," said his new friend. "They call me Sid. What's your name?"

"I'm Eddie Wilson," said Eddie. "What did you do to your head?"

"Cut it open," replied Sidney. "You should have seen the blood! Buckets of it. Had to get a crew cut."

This is a real guy! thought Eddie. Out loud he said, "I live next door."

"That's swell!" said Sidney. "Want to help me carry these boxes in the house?"

"Sure!" Eddie replied, and he set to work piling up the hatboxes.

Sidney lifted a pile of books out of the car. "These are all mine. I like to read," said Sidney. "Want to help me carry these books in?"

"I'm carrying the hatboxes," said Eddie, juggling the pile as he started up the drive toward the house. Sidney followed with a chimney of books.

At the door, Eddie met Sidney's mother. "Hello!" she called out.

"Mum," said Sidney, "this is Eddie Wilson. He lives next door."

"Why, how nice," said Mrs. Stewart. "I'm glad to meet you, Eddie. Just take those hatboxes right up to Sid's room. They're full of Sid's junk."

Eddie climbed the stairs with the boxes, thrilled to know that he was carrying Sid's junk. He could hardly wait to see what was inside of those boxes.

"My room is right here at the top of the stairs," Sidney said. "Put 'em on the floor. Want to help me put these books in the bookshelves?"

"Sure!" replied Eddie, straightening up. Then he said, "Sid, do you collect valuable property?"

"Valuable property?" said Sidney. "Do you mean treasures?"

"That's it," said Eddie. "All kinds of swell stuff."

"I sure do," replied Sidney. "Almost the whole station wagon is full of my stuff."

Eddie looked at Sidney as though Sidney had suddenly turned into Santa Claus. "Oh, Sid!" exclaimed Eddie. "That's super! I sure am lucky to have you come to live next door to me."

"You mean you have treasures too?" said Sidney.

"Yep!" said Eddie. "Piles of them."

"Well, what do you know!" said Sidney. "Do you have any animals?"

"Oh, yes!" said Eddie. "I've got a parrot, Louella, and a pony. Once I had a goat, Gardenia. She was a swell goat. And I had a snake, Percy."

"Well, wait till you see all I have," said Sidney.

The books were on the shelves now, and the children ran downstairs and out to the car. Sidney's mother had removed all of the brushes, mops, and brooms, but the station wagon still looked very full.

"Nearly all of this is my stuff," said Sidney.

Eddie whistled. "Where are you going to put it all?"

"Oh, my father says I can keep it in the basement. He's going to have a workshop there. 'Course, not the livestock."

"Livestock!" exclaimed Eddie. " What do you mean, 'livestock'? They have livestock on a ranch. I know all about ranches, 'cause I was on my Uncle Ed's ranch in Texas once."

"Well, that's what Pappy calls all my fish and animals and everything."

"Who's Pappy?" asked Eddie.

"My father," replied Sidney. "I always call him Pappy. Where's your pony?"

"I have to keep him out on our farm in the country," Eddie replied.

"Will you let me go and ride him sometime?" said Sidney.

"Sure!" replied Eddie. Then he said, "Don't you have any brothers or sisters?"

"Nope," replied Sidney, who was climbing into the car now. "Here, Eddie, you carry Napoleon." Sidney handed out two jars.

"Who's Napoleon?" Eddie asked.

"My fighting fish," replied Sidney.

"I sure want to see him," said Eddie. "What else have you got?"

"I've got two hamsters," said Sidney. "Anyway, I had two when we packed the car. Maybe I've got more now. Hamsters are always having babies. And I have a cute little lizard."

"You have?" said Eddie. "Well, say, Sid! This is the luckiest day of my life."

"Why?" asked Sidney.

"Because you moved next door to me," Eddie answered.

Sidney looked pleased. Sidney even blushed.

It took most of the morning for Sidney and Eddie to carry all the boxes, jars, crates, cartons, and odd treasures of all sizes and shapes into the house. Finally there was nothing left in the station wagon but a small-sized trunk. "These are my toys," said Sidney, pushing the trunk out. "Take one end, will you, Eddie?"

Eddie took hold of one end and together the children carried the trunk into the house. It was quite heavy, so one of the moving men carried it upstairs

and into Sidney's room.

"I'll show you my toys," said Sidney. But just as

Sidney was about to open the trunk, Eddie heard his mother calling him.

"I'm coming, Mama," Eddie called back. Then he said to Sidney, "I'm sorry, Sid, but I gotta go get my lunch now. But I'll be back."

"Okay!" said Sidney. "So long. Thanks for helping me."

"I'll be back," Eddie called, as he ran out the front door.

"Oh, Mama!" Eddie cried, as he rushed into his own house. "You should see the valuable property the fellow next door has! And three dogs, Mama, and hamsters and lizards and a fighting fish and all kinds of swell stuff! I sure am lucky to have a fellow like that move next door."

Eddie's mother looked surprised. "Why, I didn't know they had a boy in the family. I thought they only had a little girl named Sidney."

Eddie looked at his mother. "Sure, his name's Sidney," said Eddie, "but he's not a girl."

"Eddie, you're mistaken," said his mother. "Sidney is a girl's name as well as a boy's name. I was talking to Mrs. Stewart this morning and I am sure I remember her saying how nice she thought you were to help her little girl move all of her things into the house."

"Little girl!" shouted Eddie. "She can't be a girl. I won't let her be a girl."

"Eddie," said his mother, "I'm afraid you can't do anything about it. Sidney is a girl."

"Well, what is she doing with a crew cut, if she's a girl?" said Eddie.

"Her mother said that Sidney cut her head and they had to cut her hair off."

Eddie walked up and down the room. "What does she mean by wearing shirts like mine and jeans like mine and having all that swell stuff!" he shouted. "She ought to be ashamed of herself."

"Be quiet, Eddie," said his mother. "I'm sure you'll have wonderful times together."

Eddie would not listen. Instead he shouted, "Sidney Stewart! Sidney Stewart! Kidney stew, that's what she is! Kidney stew—worse than poison!"

And all afternoon Sidney Stewart wondered why Eddie Wilson did not come back to help her unpack her toys. Finally she decided to do it herself. She lifted the lid of her trunk and looked down at her beautiful dolls, all laid out on top of the pile of toys. She picked up a boy doll dressed in a Spanish bullfighter's costume. She looked at him and said, "Desidero, I'm going to change your name to Eddie."

CHAPTER 2

EDDIE'S BOA CONSTRICTOR

IT WAS not until Eddie reached the breakfast table the following day that he remembered his new friend, Sidney Stewart. His mother had just placed a plate full of pancakes in front of him when he heard Sidney's voice calling, "Eddie! Eddie!"

"Don't let her in! Don't let her in!" Eddie cried. But Sidney was already coming in the back door.

Eddie heard her coming. He slid like a seal out of his chair and under the table. He got as far away from his own chair as possible, all the way over to the side of the table where the twins' legs hung down.

"Where's Eddie?" asked Sidney.

"He just left," said Rudy.

"Where did he go?" Sidney asked.

The twins giggled.

"Guess he just thought of something," said Rudy. "He left in an awful hurry."

The twins giggled again. Joe began to kick his legs around under the table. Eddie reached out and pinched one of his legs.

"Ouch!" cried Joe. "He pinched me."

"Frank! Behave yourself," said his father.

"I didn't do a thing to him," said Frank.

"Have some pancakes, Sidney," said Rudy. "Eddie didn't touch these. They're awful good."

"Oh, thank you," said Sidney, and she climbed up on Eddie's chair.

Eddie sat on the floor. He looked around him. Three pairs of legs in Sunday trousers and one pair in blue jeans showed under the table. His father's sturdy legs were at one end, and his mother's tweed skirt was at the other end.

"Here's the butter, Sidney," he heard Rudy say.

"Thanks!" said Sidney.

Then came Rudy's voice again. "Have some maple syrup, Sidney."

"Thanks!" replied Sidney. "They're wonderful pancakes."

Eddie could feel himself getting madder and madder and hungrier and hungrier. The idea of a girl eating his pancakes! The nerve of her! He felt as hungry as a bear. Sunday-morning breakfast was his favorite breakfast. And those twins! What was so

29

funny? They couldn't stop giggling. He felt like bit-
ing their legs.

Then he heard Joe's voice. "May I have some more
pancakes, Mama?"

His mother got up and went into the kitchen. He
heard the pancake batter sizzle as she poured it on the
griddle. Then he could smell the pancakes cooking. He
thought he had never smelled anything better. Now

he could hear the scrape of the pancake turner as his mother flipped each cake over.

In a few minutes she was back. "Dad," she said, "do you want some more?"

"I certainly do," said Father. Eddie heard the pancakes being placed on his father's plate. One, two, three.

"Two for me, please," said Joe. Two went to Joe.

"Frank?" said his mother.

"Please," said Frank. Two to Frank.

"One left," said Mother. "Sidney, how about you?"

"Yes, please," said Sidney. Another pancake to Sidney.

Eddie didn't think he could stand it another minute. He looked up at the underside of the table. There was a tiny shelf that ran around the edge of the table. Eddie saw a crust of bread on the shelf right in front of Joe. Joe had evidently hidden it there once upon a time. Eddie reached up and took the crust of bread off the shelf. He examined it. It looked rather dusty, but Eddie was hungry. He put it between his teeth. It was as hard as a rock. Must have been a long time ago when Joe put this crust under the table, thought Eddie. He put the crust back on the shelf. And just then he saw his father's hand hanging down under the table. In his fingers was a pancake.

Eddie crawled over to his father and took the pancake. He wolfed it down. There was no maple syrup on it, but he was so hungry that it tasted good anyway. In a moment his father's hand appeared again with another pancake. Eddie gobbled it up and then a third appeared.

Eddie had just finished his third pancake when he heard his mother say, "Come, boys, it's time for you to go to Sunday School." At the same moment he heard Sidney's mother calling her.

Sidney got down from Eddie's chair and said, "Thanks for the good breakfast."

In a moment Eddie heard the back door close. He came out from his hiding place. "Thanks, Dad!" he said. "Those pancakes saved my life."

"Hurry, boys," said Mrs. Wilson, who was already clearing the table. The three older boys dashed upstairs. Eddie picked up the bottle of maple syrup and took a big gulp.

"Eddie!" his mother cried. "What do you mean by drinking the maple syrup?"

"Well, Mama, I didn't get any maple syrup on my pancakes," said Eddie. "Can't I have my maple syrup? That Stewpot from next door got my pancakes and maple syrup and everything."

The rest of the day Eddie ducked in and out of the house. He didn't want to meet Sidney. But in the afternoon he heard her calling, "Eddie! Eddie!"

Eddie was in his room. When he heard his mother say, "Hello, Sidney," Eddie crawled under his bed. With his heart beating in his throat, he heard Sidney say, "Is Eddie home?"

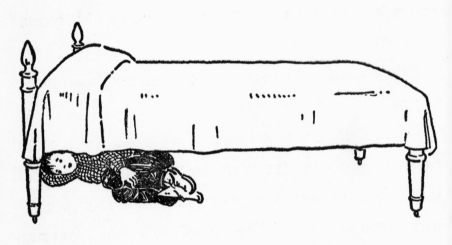

"I think he's up in his room," said Mother.

Eddie crawled as far back under the bed as he could, for now he could hear Sidney's feet stomping up the stairs. He held his breath. Now he could see her feet in the doorway. Sneakers! Sneakers, just like his own, were sticking out from under blue jeans. It was hard to believe that those feet belonged to a girl. Eddie shut his eyes tight. He was sure that if he didn't see those feet the owner of the feet wouldn't see him. In a few moments he heard Sidney's feet going downstairs. Then her voice said, "Eddie isn't in his room."

"I guess he's gone out," said Mother.

Eddie opened his eyes and crawled out from under the bed.

At supper Eddie was alone with his father and mother. Rudy and the twins had gone to watch a ball game. For dessert Mrs. Wilson placed half a coconut-cream pie on the table. It was left over from Saturday night's dinner. Eddie loved coconut-cream pie. It was his favorite pie. He watched his mother cut three pieces and noticed that there was a nice piece left on the plate.

When he finished eating his pie he looked at the piece on the pie plate and said, "Mama, may I . . ."

But that was as far as he got before he heard Sidney's voice again. This time it was at the back door. "Eddie! Eddie!" she called.

Eddie jumped up like a jack rabbit and, with what appeared to be two leaps, landed inside the coat closet in the hall.

For the third time that day he heard his mother's voice say, "Hello, Sidney."

"Is Eddie home yet?" asked Sidney.

"He just this minute left," Father said.

Then, to his horror, he heard his mother say, "Sidney, wouldn't you like to have this piece of coconut-cream pie?"

"Oh, yes, thank you," said Sidney.

"Well, sit right up here in Eddie's place," said Mother.

Eddie heard his chair being pulled out. Then Sidney's voice said, "Thank you."

She sure is an eater, thought Eddie. Doesn't she ever eat anything in her own house?

Eddie sat down on the floor of the closet. As he did so he knocked over his father's golf clubs. They fell to the floor with a terrible clatter.

"Humph!" said Mr. Wilson. "Must be Eddie's boa constrictor thrashing around in the closet. Eddie must have forgotten to feed it again." Mr. Wilson got up. "Guess I better let him out and give him his dinner."

Now Sidney knew what a boa constrictor was. She had seen one at the zoo. It was the biggest snake in the zoo. She had seen it swallow a whole little pig. It was very interesting to watch as long as the boa constrictor was behind glass, but Sidney didn't ever want to meet one personally. She liked animals, but not boa constrictors.

Sidney laid down the fork she had picked up to eat the pie with and said, "I think I hear my mother calling me." She was out the back door before Mr. Wilson had reached the coat closet. When he opened the door he said, "Come out, Eddie. She's gone."

Eddie came out. "Phew!" he said. "It's hot in there."

"Come have another piece of pie," said his father.

Eddie sat down in his chair, picked up the fork that Sidney had dropped, and ate the pie. "How did you get rid of her, Dad?" said Eddie.

"Oh, I just said that I guessed I would have to feed your boa constrictor that you kept in the coat closet. That did it. Sidney evidently doesn't like boa constrictors." Eddie and his father laughed.

Mrs. Wilson looked at Eddie's father and said, "You should be ashamed of yourself, making up a story like that to scare a little girl."

"*She* should be ashamed of herself," said Mr. Wilson. "She's had poor Eddie here scared all day. If she could be a make-believe boy yesterday, why can't we have a make-believe boa constrictor today? Turn about is fair play."

"You're a pal, Dad! The best pal a fellow ever had," said Eddie, as he scraped up the last of the coconut-cream pie.

CHAPTER 3

THE PRINTING PRESS

EDDIE was glad to go back to school on Monday morning. He was glad to get away from the house and his new neighbor, Sidney Stewart. On his way to school he stopped at the drugstore to buy a notebook. As he was leaving the store, a sign caught Eddie's eye. It said *Come and get it!* Eddie was always interested in signs, and he was especially interested in anything that he could go and get; so he stopped to read the sign. His eyes grew larger as he read. *Will give away an old printing press to anyone who will take it away.* Underneath was the name and address of the Rialto Printing Company, 2nd and Green Streets, and the words *Open evenings.*

Eddie knew exactly where the Rialto Printing Company was. He had passed it many times. He decided then and there that he would go and get the printing press. Then he thought that as long as he was going to get it, the fewer people that saw the sign the better. Nobody was paying any attention to him, so he pulled out the four thumbtacks that held up the sign. He turned it wrong side out and pinned it up again. Now it was just a blank white card. Eddie was about to open the door when he decided that it was a shame to have a sign with nothing on it, so he went back, and with a piece of black crayon that he found in his pocket he printed on it *Don't slam the door!*

Eddie ran off to school thinking about his printing press. He had wanted a printing press for a long time, ever since he had spent a day with his Uncle Bill, who had a small hand press. It was a real press, not a toy. Uncle Bill had taught Eddie how to set the type and operate the press. He had printed cards the whole afternoon for Uncle Bill.

Now he was going to have a press of his own. He could hardly believe it. A printing press! Now he would publish a paper. And he would sell copies all over the neighborhood. He began to think about a name for his paper. By the time he reached school, he had decided to call it *Hot News.*

He rushed into the classroom with his thoughts full of the newspaper, but they were blown right out of his head when he saw Sidney Stewart standing by the teacher's desk. She was shaking hands with Miss Rice.

There she stood in a blue-and-white striped dress. Instead of the bandage, she was wearing a wide red ribbon around her head. Eddie couldn't bear to look at her. She looked just the way his friends Boodles Cary and Dumpty Peterson would look if they were dressed in girls' dresses and red ribbons.

Miss Rice looked up and saw Eddie. "Why, here's Eddie now!" she said. "Eddie, Sidney tells me that she lives next door to you and that you are very good friends."

Eddie's face turned bright red and he just grunted.

"That is not a very pleasant way to say good morning," said Miss Rice.

"Good morning," Eddie said.

"Now, Sidney," said Miss Rice, "I think it would be nice for you to sit in the seat in front of Eddie. The boy who sat there has just moved away."

Eddie groaned, but Sidney looked pleased as she sat

down in the vacant seat directly in front of him.

Anna Patricia, who sat across the aisle from Sidney, watched her as she settled herself. She liked Sidney's schoolbag. It was black shiny leather trimmed with red—not plaid like every other bag in the room. She saw her take out a pencil box. It matched the bag and when Sidney opened it, Anna Patricia saw that it was filled with bright red pencils. And she had a red notebook, just like the one that Anna Patricia had bought that morning in the drugstore.

Anna Patricia leaned across the aisle and said, "Where did you get that red notebook?"

"At the drugstore," said Sidney.

Anna Patricia held up her notebook and said, "I've got one too."

When the bell rang for school to begin, Miss Rice said, "Boys and girls, this is Sidney Stewart. Will you please say good morning to Sidney?"

Everyone in the class turned to look at Sidney. Then all of the children sang out, "Good morning, Sidney." Sidney said, "Good morning."

Boodles, who sat in the center of the room where everyone could see him, pointed to his hair, which was cut in a crew cut, and made a funny face. The children knew that he was poking fun at Sidney's hair-cut. They began to giggle.

"I do not like your behavior, Boswell Cary," said Miss Rice.

Boodles always knew when Miss Rice was displeased with him, because then she called him by his real name, Boswell.

"Sidney had to have her hair cut off," said Miss Rice, "because she cut her head."

Everyone turned and looked at Sidney with more interest than ever.

At recess Boodles Cary sang out, "Eddie's got a girl friend! Eddie's got a girl friend! Sidney Stewart! Sidney Stewart!"

"She's no friend of mine," said Eddie.

"She said she was," Dumpty Peterson shouted. "I heard her."

"Well, she isn't," said Eddie, "and she never will be.

46

I wouldn't be a friend of hers, not if you gave me a spaceship. The old Stewpot!"

All through recess Anna Patricia stuck to Sidney. "Don't you mind, Sidney," she said, "if they make fun of your hair. They used to make fun of me because I didn't have any front teeth, but now they're all jealous because I'm the only one in the whole school that can take my teeth out."

This news was a great surprise to Sidney, and she was even more surprised when Anna Patricia pulled out her two lower front teeth.

"That's wonderful," said Sidney.

"My father made them for me," said Anna Patricia. "My father is a dentist. You ought to get a wig, Sidney. Then you could take your hair off and they would all be jealous of you."

Sidney thought this over. Then she said, "But where can I get a wig?"

"Maybe at some hairdresser's," said Anna Patricia.

"But that would cost a lot of money," said Sidney.

Anna Patricia wrinkled up her forehead. She was thinking. Then she said, "Maybe Eddie Wilson has one."

"What would Eddie Wilson be doing with a wig?" Sidney asked.

"Oh, Eddie has all kinds of stuff," said Anna Patricia. "He collects everything. He even has two of my old teeth."

"I collect things too," said Sidney.

"What kind of things?" Anna Patricia asked.

"Oh, all kinds of treasures," said Sidney. "And animals. But I don't have any wig."

"Eddie Wilson has wonderful stuff," said Anna Patricia. "Do you have very much?"

"Well, it almost filled our station wagon," said Sidney proudly.

Anna Patricia looked at Sidney with admiring eyes. Then she said rather slowly, "I think I'll start collecting things. I think I will."

Just then the bell rang for the children to return to their classrooms. At the door, Anna Patricia met Eddie. "Oh, Eddie!" she said. "Do you have a wig that Sidney Stewart could have. She needs a wig awful badly. Just look at her head."

"No, I haven't," said Eddie, and he brushed past Anna Patricia.

"Oh, Eddie, I wish you had," said Sidney.

"Don't bother me," said Eddie.

It was hard for Eddie to keep his thoughts on his reading lesson, because he kept thinking about the printing press he was going to get. He could hardly wait to go for it. He hoped his father wouldn't be busy after dinner. Eddie was going to ask him to drive him over to the Rialto Printing Company, so that he could pick up the printing press. He wondered how big it would be. Maybe they would need a truck. Eddie began to think about how he could get a truck. He was so busy thinking about it that he did not hear Miss Rice say, "Eddie, will you continue, please."

Miss Rice said it again, and Eddie jumped. "Continue, Eddie," said Miss Rice.

Eddie stood up with his book. He had no idea what he was to continue. He frowned and looked all over the page.

"Eddie," said Miss Rice, "I am afraid you have not been paying attention. If you lose the place again, you will remain after school." Then she said, "Sidney, will you continue, please."

Sidney jumped. Then she picked up her book and stood beside her desk. She, too, looked all over the page.

"Sidney," said Miss Rice, "have you been dreaming

too, just like Eddie? What have you been thinking about?"

"I'm sorry," said Sidney. "I was thinking about something I'm going to get tonight."

Humph! thought Eddie. Just like me. Only she isn't going to get what I'm going to get.

"Well," said Miss Rice, "as this is your first day, Sidney, I'll ask Anna Patricia to show you the place."

Anna Patricia stood up and pointed to the place in Sidney's book, and Sidney began to read.

As soon as school was over, Eddie dashed home at top speed. He ran to his mother and said, "Mama! I'm going to get a printing press. Isn't that wonderful, Mama? The Rialto Printing Company is giving it away. All I have to do is go and get it. Do you think Dad can take me over after dinner to get it?"

"I don't know," said his mother. "You'll have to ask him when he comes home."

"Well, don't tell the boys," said Eddie. "I want to surprise them."

"Very well," replied Mrs. Wilson.

Eddie went out front to watch for his father. He was glad Sidney was not around. He had seen enough of her at school. Every once in a while he could hear her voice calling to her mother. It seemed to come from the basement. Once he heard her call, "Mum, will you please help me move something?"

Pushing her stuff around, I guess, Eddie thought. And for a moment Eddie began to wonder what was in all those boxes and cartons that he had helped Sidney carry into the basement. Oh, well! He didn't care. Probably just a lot of junk. Not valuable property like mine, thought Eddie.

Now he could hear Sidney's voice again. "Mum, I want to move all this so that I can put it right here."

Eddie couldn't help wondering what she was going

to put "right here." Oh, probably some old truck, he said to himself. He was sure Sidney wouldn't know valuable property if she saw it.

Just then his father came around the corner. Eddie set off at top speed. When he reached his father he said, "Dad! Dad! Will you help me? Will you? I gotta go get a printing press, Dad. Over at the Rialto Printing Company—you know. They're giving it away, Dad, and I'm going to get it. Isn't that super? A real printing press! I'm going to publish a paper. I'm going to call it *Hot News*."

Eddie was just finishing his dessert when he heard the Stewarts' station wagon back out of their driveway, but he thought nothing of that. As soon as his father rose from his chair at the table, Eddie said, "Can we go now, Dad?"

Eddie's brothers looked up. "Where you going?" Rudy asked.

"What's up?" said Joe.

"What's the mystery?" asked Frank.

"Dad and I are going to get something," replied Eddie. "You'll see it when we come back."

"You and your mysteries!" said Joe, as Eddie rushed out the door.

Eddie was already settled on the front seat when his father reached the car. "Dad," he said, "do you think we can put it in the trunk of the car? Maybe we should try to borrow a truck."

"If it's too big to go in the trunk, it's too big to go in our house," said his father.

"Oh, I don't think it will be too big to go in the trunk," said Eddie. "I'll bet it's just a nice little printing press."

"Well, it had better be a nice little one," said his father. "Are you sure this place is open in the evening?"

"Oh, yes!" said Eddie. "It said on the sign *Open evenings.*"

Mr. Wilson drove into the parking space behind the Rialto Printing Company. The windows were lighted, and Eddie could see men moving around inside. He jumped out of the car the moment it stopped, and galloped up to the door. He pulled it open and walked inside.

"Hello, son," said a man at a desk.

"I've come for the printing press," said Eddie cheerfully.

"Well, I'm sorry, Bud," said the man, "but somebody just drove off with it."

"Drove off with it!" exclaimed Eddie. He could hardly believe it.

"Yes. We just gave it away," said the man.

"But, but," Eddie stammered, "I wanted it myself."

"That's too bad," said the man. "You should have come sooner. Gave it to a little girl, not more than ten minutes ago."

Eddie let out a yell. "I know her! I know her!" he cried. "You don't have to tell me. That Stewpot again!"

Mr. Wilson put his arm around Eddie's shoulders. "Now, Eddie," he said, "quiet down. It can't be helped. Maybe there will be another one around before long."

"This one was just a little hand press," said the printer.

"But that's just what I want," Eddie wailed. "A nice little hand press."

Eddie and his father got back into the car. Eddie could hardly keep the tears back. He had to blink his eyes very hard, and there was a lump in his throat that felt like a baseball. He muttered to himself, "What's a girl want with a printing press anyway? Just ten minutes, and I would have got there first. I heard them back their station wagon out of the drive. I might have known!"

"Maybe she'll let you use it," said his father. "She seems like a nice girl."

"I don't want to use her old printing press," said Eddie. "I don't even want to look at it."

When Eddie reached home he ran right up to his room, shut the door, and threw himself on the bed. In a moment he heard Sidney's voice under his window calling, "Eddie! Eddie!"

Eddie got up and hastily pulled down the window shade.

Soon his mother came into the room, carrying a plate. On the plate was a piece of chocolate cake. "Eddie," she said, "I thought you might like a piece of chocolate cake."

Eddie's voice, smothered in the pillow, could just be heard. "No, thank you, Mama."

"Sidney was calling you," said his mother. "I wonder what she wanted."

Eddie made no sign that he heard.

"Well," said his mother, "if you don't want the chocolate cake, I guess I'll take it downstairs."

Eddie sat up. He reached for the plate. "I guess I could eat a little bit of it," he said.

Mrs. Wilson sat down in the chair in front of Eddie's desk. She watched him as he ate the chocolate cake. He seemed to be thinking deeply. As he swallowed the last piece and scraped up a crumb of icing from the plate, he said, "Mama, where do you think I could get a nice wig?"

"A wig?" said his mother.

"Yes—you know," said Eddie. "What you wear on your head."

"What color wig?" asked Mrs. Wilson.

"Well, sort of red," said Eddie.

"I don't know," said his mother, "but I'll think about it."

CHAPTER 4

A FELLOW HAS TO RIDE AROUND

THE next morning when Eddie reached school, Sidney said, "Oh, Eddie! I've got the most wonderful thing!"

"I know! I know!" said Eddie.

"Did my mother tell you?" said Sidney.

"She didn't have to tell me," said Eddie. "I know

all about it." And he went to the back of the room and began to nail two pieces of wood together.

When Anna Patricia arrived, Eddie saw her rush up to Sidney. Soon they were both chattering like two excited sparrows. Eddie knew Anna Patricia well. She always talked about everything as though it was the most exciting thing that had ever happened, even though she had only broken her fingernail or found a little old stub of a lead pencil. Everything was hot news to Anna Patricia, thought Eddie. That reminded him of the newspaper he had planned to publish, and he felt very bad again. He pounded the nails harder than ever.

The week passed by. Sidney sat in front of Eddie, but Eddie paid no attention to her. He did not pay any attention to Anna Patricia either. Several times Anna Patricia tried to talk to him, but each time Eddie ran off. He just wouldn't listen to either Sidney or Anna Patricia. He was sick of girls. Let them gabble together, thought Eddie. They're always gabbling.

Once he heard Anna Patricia say to Sidney, "It's a shame you can't find a wig anyplace. It must be awful not to have much hair. I know how I felt when I didn't have any teeth. I felt just awful."

Then he heard Sidney's reply. "Oh, yes! I'd give anything I have for a wig."

When Eddie got home from school that day, he said to his mother, "Mama, have you had any luck finding a wig?"

"Not yet," his mother replied.

"That's too bad." Eddie sighed.

On Saturday, right after breakfast, Mrs. Wilson said, "Eddie, this morning I'd like you to take a package over to Mrs. West, the dressmaker. You can go over on your bicycle."

"Oh, Mama!" said Eddie. "Do I have to? I got a

lot to do this morning. Why can't one of the twins take it over?"

"The twins are raking leaves for Mrs. Turner, down the street," said his mother. "What do you have to do that is so important?"

"I gotta ride around on my bike," said Eddie. "It's Saturday. I have to see what's doing. I might find some valuable property."

"You'll have plenty of time to ride around after you leave the package at Mrs. West's for me," said his mother.

"Okay," said Eddie.

Mrs. Wilson gave Eddie the package, and he went over to the garage for his bicycle. About fifteen minutes later he stopped in front of Mrs. West's house. He got off his bicycle, wheeled it up to the front steps, and leaned it against the wall of the house. Eddie rang the bell. In a moment the door was opened by a plump, white-haired woman. It was Mrs. West. "Well, I suppose you are Eddie," she said.

"Yes, I am," said Eddie. "This is the package that Mama sent you."

"Thank you, Eddie," said Mrs. West. "Won't you come in?"

"No, thanks," said Eddie. "I got a lot to do."

"Oh, that's too bad," said Mrs. West. "I just made some doughnuts. Just finished them about ten minutes ago. They're still warm. I thought you might like a couple with a glass of milk."

"Well," said Eddie, "I guess I could stop long enough to eat a doughnut, but I gotta hurry." Eddie stepped in.

"Come right back into the kitchen," said Mrs. West.

Eddie followed Mrs. West into the kitchen. It smelled like a bakery shop. Several dozen fresh, golden-brown doughnuts were spread out on white paper towels.

"I've just been rolling them in sugar," said Mrs. West, picking up two of the doughnuts and putting them on a plate. "Don't you think you'll have time to eat two?" she said.

Eddie hesitated. "I guess so," he said.

"Might as well have a glass of milk with them," said Mrs. West. "Won't take much more time."

"Thank you," said Eddie, as he took the doughnuts and the glass of milk.

"Pull up a chair and sit down, Eddie," said Mrs. West.

"Oh, I don't have time to sit down," said Eddie. "I'll just stand here. These doughnuts sure are good."

"Where are you going in such a hurry?" asked Mrs. West.

"Oh, I have an awful lot of things to do," Eddie replied.

"Errands for your mother?" said Mrs. West.

"No," said Eddie, "but I have to ride around on my bike . . . and . . . and . . . ride around. You know how it is . . . you . . . well, you gotta ride around. If you don't ride around, you don't know what's going on. A fella might miss something."

"That's right. Don't let me keep you," said Mrs. West, as she took the empty plate and glass from Eddie.

Eddie looked at the doughnuts and said, "Oh, you're not keeping me. It's very nice here. You've got a nice kitchen, haven't you?"

"I think so," replied Mrs. West.

"You sure make wonderful doughnuts," said Eddie. "Best I ever ate."

"Thank you, Eddie," said Mrs. West. "I'm glad you enjoyed them."

"Well, I guess I better go," said Eddie, not moving an inch away from the kitchen table.

"Well, Eddie, don't let me keep you," said Mrs. West.

Eddie looked longingly at the doughnuts. He sighed and said, "I sure wish . . . I sure wish I could find a wig."

Mrs. West gave a start. "A what, Eddie?" she asked him.

"A wig," said Eddie. "Thing you wear on your head when you don't have any hair."

"Oh!" said Mrs. West. "A wig!"

"Yep!" said Eddie. "If I could find a wig, I'd have a printing press."

"How very remarkable!" said Mrs. West. "Just how does a wig turn into a printing press?"

"It doesn't," replied Eddie. "But I could trade the wig for a printing press." Then Eddie sat down on the kitchen stool and told Mrs. West all about Sidney Stewart.

69

When he finished, Mrs. West said, "Eddie, I think I have a wig packed away in a chest with some costumes up in the attic."

"You have?" cried Eddie.

"I think I have," said Mrs. West. "When I was a girl I was in a lot of plays. I had all kinds of costumes, and once I had a wig. Now if you just had time, we could go up in the attic and look for it."

"Oh, Mrs. West!" Eddie cried. "I've got lots of time."

"But you said you had to ride around," said Mrs. West.

"Oh, this is just what a fella rides around for," said Eddie.

Eddie followed Mrs. West up to the attic. There she lifted a pile of boxes off a wooden chest. "Haven't opened this for years," she said, kneeling down in front of the chest. Eddie knelt down beside her as she lifted the lid. A musty odor came from the inside. "I do hope the moths haven't got into the wig," said Mrs. West.

"I hope not," said Eddie, " 'cause I don't think Sidney's mother would like it if Sidney had moths in her head."

"Probably not," said Mrs. West, lifting a blue satin dress out of the chest. As she did so she uncovered a dagger.

"Oh, look!" Eddie cried out. "A dagger!"

"Yes," said Mrs. West, handing it to Eddie.

Eddie took it carefully. "Why, it's rubber!" he exclaimed. "It looks just like real."

"You may have it, Eddie, if you like it," said Mrs. West.

"Oh, thanks!" said Eddie. "Thanks."

Eddie stuck the dagger in his belt and watched Mrs. West as she lifted more dresses out of the chest. The pile on the floor grew bigger as she neared the bottom, but no wig had been unearthed. Finally she picked up the last dress, and there lay a mussed-up wig. "There it is!" cried Mrs. West.

Eddie looked at it. It had long, straight yellow hair, and it looked as big as a bucket.

"Try it on, Eddie," said Mrs. West. "It will give you an idea how Sidney will look in it."

Eddie put it on. The bang came down over his eyes and almost touched the tip of his nose. He felt as though he were under a haystack. Eddie parted the hair and looked at himself in an old cracked mirror that was standing against the wall. He thought he looked exactly like one of those Skye terriers that win blue ribbons in dog shows. He was afraid Sidney wouldn't care to look like a Skye terrier, not even like one that won blue ribbons. "It's sort of big, isn't it?" he said.

"Oh, I can fix that," said Mrs. West. "I can just take a few tucks in it."

Eddie held the wig in his hand. "Sort of needs a permanent, doesn't it?" he said.

"It would look better if it had some curl in it," said Mrs. West. "I can do that with a curling iron."

"Sidney's hair is sort of red," said Eddie. "I don't know whether she'd like yellow hair. Maybe you could dye it? Huh? Maybe?"

"I think the first thing to do is to take some tucks in it," said Mrs. West, beginning to put all the dresses back in the chest. After she had closed the lid she and Eddie went downstairs.

Eddie sat on a chair and watched Mrs. West take tucks inside the wig. When she finished she tried it on Eddie again. Now he could see, but what he saw did not look the way he thought Sidney Stewart would want to look. The hair stood out in bunches over each ear and on top of his head.

"It will look much better when it's curled," said Mrs. West.

"Oh, sure!" said Eddie.

"Now I think we had better have some lunch," said Mrs. West.

"I guess I'd better telephone my mother," said Eddie, "and tell her that I'm not going to be home for lunch."

Eddie called his mother while Mrs. West fixed the lunch. "Mama," said Eddie, "I'm staying for lunch at Mrs. West's."

"Staying for lunch!" exclaimed his mother. "Why, Eddie! What have you and Mrs. West been doing all morning?"

"Looking for a wig. And we found one, Mama!" replied Eddie. "We found one! I gotta go now. See you later."

Eddie finished off his lunch with more doughnuts. Then Mrs. West said, "Eddie, you run down to the drugstore on the corner and get me some hair rinse for red hair."

"Wouldn't just some red ink do?" said Eddie.

"I'm afraid not," said Mrs. West.

Eddie ran to the drugstore. In a few minutes he was back with the hair rinse. He leaned against the kitchen washtub and watched Mrs. West dip the wig in a basin of reddish-brown liquid.

"Looks like root beer, doesn't it?" said Eddie. "You sure it's the right color?"

"I think it will be all right," said Mrs. West, as she lifted the dripping wig out of the basin. Eddie watched it grow lighter as it dried. When it was dry it was not quite as bright as a carrot, but it was not very far from it.

Mrs. West clipped the hair shorter here and there. Then she set to work with a curling iron. Eddie was more and more delighted with the results. When it was finished it was quite a mop of curls.

"That's super duper!" cried Eddie. "If I didn't want that printing press so much, I'd keep it. It's real valuable property."

Mrs. West put the wig in a paper bag and gave it to Eddie. As Eddie left, he said, "It was swell of you, Mrs. West, to give me this wig. Thanks for all the trouble you took, and thanks for the lunch and the doughnuts. They were terrific!"

Eddie rode home at top speed. He went right to Sidney's house. He rang the bell and Sidney came to the door. "Why, hello, Eddie!" Sidney cried. "Come on in."

"Hello, Sid," said Eddie. "Wait till you see what I have!" Eddie opened the paper bag and pulled out the wig.

Sidney's eyes grew very big as she looked at it. "Oh, Eddie!" she cried.

"Try it on," said Eddie.

Sidney tried it on. She looked like an orange poodle. "How does it look?" she said.

"Great!" said Eddie.

Sidney ran to look in the mirror. "Oh, Eddie!" she said. "It's wonderful!"

"Well, Sid," said Eddie, "if you'll give me that printing press, I'll give you the wig."

Sidney looked at Eddie for a moment. Then she said, "What printing press?"

"The one you got from the Rialto Printing place," said Eddie.

"I didn't get any printing press," said Sidney.

"You didn't?" cried Eddie.

"No," said Sidney, "but Anna Patricia got a printing press."

"Anna Patricia!" Eddie screamed. And he grabbed the wig off Sidney's head and ran out of the house.

CHAPTER 5

THE FIRST HOT NEWS

Eddie rode straight to Anna Patricia's. He did not even bother to put the wig back in the paper bag. He kept it in his hand and it hung from the handle bars like a scalp.

Anna Patricia was outside when Eddie reached her house. She was surprised to see him. "Hello, Annie Pat!" Eddie called out.

"Hello, Eddie!" said Anna Patricia. "What's that you have in your hand?"

"It's a wig!" said Eddie, holding it up.

Anna Patricia's face lighted up with pleasure. "Oh, Eddie!" she cried. "I think you're wonderful! Can I have it? I'd like to give it to Sidney. It's just right for Sidney."

Eddie did not reply. Instead he stuffed the wig inside of his shirt.

"Oh!" cried Anna Patricia. "You'll muss it all up, and it's so beautiful!"

Eddie spread his feet apart and put his hands on his hips. "Annie Pat," he said, "have you got that printing press?"

"Oh, yes!" said Anna Patricia. "It's wonderful, Eddie! I've been trying all week to tell you about it, only you wouldn't listen to me."

"Well, I didn't know you had that printing press,"

said Eddie. "What are you going to do with a printing press?"

"Oh, I'm collecting treasures, like you and Sidney," replied Anna Patricia.

Eddie held his head. "This is awful!" he cried. "Everybody collecting valuable property. There isn't going to be enough valuable property for everybody. And, anyway, girls shouldn't collect the things that boys collect. It isn't fair. Why don't you collect dolls?"

"That's a good idea, Eddie!" said Anna Patricia. "I think I will. That's an awfully good idea, Eddie. I don't have very many. Where do you think I could find some?"

"Find some?" said Eddie. "What do you mean, 'find some'?"

"Well, Eddie, you find things all the time," said Anna Patricia.

"But not dolls," said Eddie.

"Well, if you don't find dolls, how do you expect me to find dolls?" said Anna Patricia.

"But I don't want to find dolls," said Eddie.

"Oh, I think you're mean," said Anna Patricia. "You tell me to collect dolls and then you won't tell me where to find them. I'm not going to show you my printing press."

"Listen, Annie Pat," said Eddie. "Here's what I'll do. If you'll show me the printing press, I'll give you the first doll I find."

Anna Patricia thought about this for a moment. Then she said, "All right."

"Where is it?" Eddie asked.

"In the garage," said Anna Patricia.

"What have you been printing on it?" Eddie inquired.

"Nothing," replied Anna Patricia. "It makes my hands dirty."

"Makes your hands dirty!" exclaimed Eddie. "Well, what are you doing with it?"

"Nothing," said Anna Patricia. "I just like to look at it. It's my first treasure. Come on, I'll show it to you."

Anna Patricia and Eddie went into the garage. There stood the printing press on a wooden box. It was just the kind that Eddie wanted.

Eddie looked it all over. Then he said, "Annie Pat, if you'll give me this printing press, I'll give you this wig."

"But I don't want a wig," said Anna Patricia. "Sidney wants a wig."

"You could give it to Sidney," said Eddie.

"But if I gave the printing press to you and I gave the wig to Sidney, I wouldn't have any treasure at all," said Anna Patricia.

"Tell you what, Annie Pat," said Eddie. "I'll give

84

you the wig and this rubber dagger." Eddie pulled the dagger from his belt and handed it to Anna Patricia.

Anna Patricia looked at it. Then she handed it back to Eddie. "No, thank you," she said. "I'm collecting dolls."

"Annie Pat!" cried Eddie. "You can't have a printing press and not print with it."

"Yes, I can," said Anna Patricia. "But, Eddie, if you want to print with my printing press you can print here."

"I want to do it at home," Eddie wailed. "Tell you what, Annie Pat. If I find a doll for you, will you give me the printing press?"

Anna Patricia thought about this offer for a minute. Then she said, "Well, if it was nice enough, maybe I would."

"But I can't wait," Eddie argued. "I want to publish a paper."

"Oh, Eddie!" exclaimed Anna Patricia. "I think that would be wonderful! Let's do it together."

"Girls don't publish papers," said Eddie.

"They do! They do!" cried Anna Patricia. "Anyway, ladies do. I know they do. My mother told me they do."

"Okay! Okay!" said Eddie. "But you'll have to work. You'll have to go around and get all the news on this street, and it has to be good. I'm going to call this newspaper *Hot News.*"

"Oh, Eddie! That's wonderful!" said Anna Patricia.

"And you have to go out and sell it," said Eddie.

"On the street corner?" said Anna Patricia.

"No," replied Eddie, "just to our customers. They have to subscribe."

"What do you mean, 'subscribe'?" Anna Patricia asked.

"They have to pay twenty-five cents a month and they get the paper every Saturday," said Eddie.

"Oh!" said Anna Patricia. "Who's going to get the twenty-five cents?"

Eddie had to think about this question a few minutes. Then he said, "We'll divide it. But you have to work. You have to get subscriptions and you have to get news."

"All right," said Anna Patricia. "How do I get the news?"

"You have to go around to all the neighbors and ask, 'What's the news in your family?'" said Eddie.

"Oh!" said Anna Patricia. "I'd like that."

All the time Eddie and Anna Patricia were talking, Eddie was busy setting type. Now he was ready to print, but he did not have any paper. "Can you get some paper, Annie Pat?" he asked.

"I'll see," said Anna Patricia.

Anna Patricia went into the house and came back with a roll of white paper. "My mother says we can have this end of her shelf paper," she said.

"That's swell," said Eddie. "Have you got any scissors?"

Anna Patricia went off for scissors. When she returned with the scissors, Eddie said, "Say, Annie Pat, have you got any ink?"

"Oh, yes!" said Anna Patricia. "The man gave me some. That's what makes your hands so dirty. It's just like black tooth paste." Anna Patricia handed the tube over to Eddie, and he squeezed some black paste onto the printing press. He put a sheet of paper down and in a moment he held up his first printed sheet. It said: "Important Noncement! New Nayborhood Paper! Hot News! Published every Saturday by Edward Wilson. Scription price $.25 a month."

Anna Patricia read it. "You haven't got my name

on it," she cried. "I won't let you print on my printing press if you don't put my name on it. It's our paper. It's our business. It has got to have my name on it."

"Aw, Annie Pat!" said Eddie. But he set to work with the type again. Then he ran another piece of paper through. He had added: "Anna Patricia Wallace, Head Reporter." Anna Patricia was as pleased as Punch.

"Now remember, Annie Pat, you have to get some exciting news. We only print exciting news."

"Okay!" said Anna Patricia.

When Eddie reached home, he found Sidney sitting on the stone wall. "Hello, Eddie!" she said. "Did you see Anna Patricia?"

"Yep!" said Eddie. Then he held out the wig. "Here," he said, "you can have it."

Sidney took the wig and said, "Oh, Eddie! Thank

you!" She put it on and looked at Eddie. "How does it look?" she asked.

Eddie could never have believed that a wig could make anyone look so different. She reminded him of the clown, Lollipop, that he had seen in the circus last May. "It's a little mussed up," he said.

All during the following week Eddie and Anna Patricia went to their neighbors' houses to get subscriptions for *Hot News,* and at each house they asked, "Got any exciting news?"

By Thursday they had eleven subscriptions—two dollars and seventy-five cents. "That's a dollar and thirty-seven-and-a-half cents each," said Anna Patricia.

"Have you got any exciting news?" Eddie asked her.

Anna Patricia took a piece of paper out of her pocket. She read off the news: "Mrs. Smith's baby has a tooth. Mrs. Black's dog is going to have puppies, she thinks. The Robinsons' cat caught a mouse. Bobby Taylor lost his boat down the sewer."

"Annie Pat!" cried Eddie. "That isn't exciting news!"

"Well, what have you got?" inquired Anna Patricia.

Eddie took out a piece of paper. "Well," he said, "I haven't got so very much yet, but it's only Thursday."

"Well, what *have* you got?" said Anna Patricia.

Eddie cleared his throat. "The firemen of Company 3 had a false alarm on Tuesday afternoon at 4.10 P.M.," he read.

"What else?" said Anna Patricia.

"It's only Thursday," said Eddie.

"Humph!" said Anna Patricia, tossing her head, and she walked off.

On Friday morning when Anna Patricia woke up, she looked down from her bedroom window to the kitchen roof of the house next door, where Mr. and

Mrs. Smith lived. To her great surprise, there was a large bird standing on the roof. Anna Patricia had never seen such a big bird on any roof before. It had

a very long tail, which trailed behind it like the train on a lady's ball dress.

Anna Patricia, still in her nightgown, ran downstairs to her mother. "Mummie!" she cried. "Come see! Come see! There's a great big bird on the roof next door."

"I'm busy with breakfast now, Anna Patricia," said her mother. "I haven't time to look at a bird. What kind of bird is it?"

"I don't know," said Anna Patricia. "It's a great big bird. I guess it's a turkey."

"Nonsense!" said her mother. "There are no wild turkeys around here."

Suddenly there was a piercing scream. Anna Patricia jumped, and her mother dropped an egg on the kitchen floor. "What was that?" her mother cried, and they both rushed to the kitchen door. There was another screech. It came from the Smiths' roof.

Mrs. Wallace looked up. When she saw the bird she exclaimed, "Why, I believe it's a peacock!"

"A peacock!" said Anna Patricia. "I never saw a live peacock before."

At that moment Mr. and Mrs. Smith came out of their kitchen door. When they saw Anna Patricia and her mother, Mr. Smith said, "What was that terrible screeching? It's enough to curdle your blood."

"You seem to have an unusual visitor," said Mrs. Wallace. "There's a peacock on your roof."

"A peacock!" said Mr. and Mrs. Smith in chorus. "How could a peacock get on our roof?" said Mrs. Smith. "I never saw one before in my life," said Mr. Smith. "I didn't even know that the creatures could fly."

"I didn't know it either," said Anna Patricia's mother, "but that certainly can't be anything except a peacock."

THE FIRST HOT NEWS

Mr. and Mrs. Smith looked up at the peacock. "I thought only storks landed on people's roofs," said Mr. Smith, "and not in this country."

"What shall we do?" said Mrs. Smith.

Mrs. Wallace laughed. "I don't know," she said, "but I do know that I have to clean up the egg I dropped on the floor and, Anna Patricia, you have to run upstairs and get dressed for school."

Anna Patricia took a long time getting dressed, because she kept running to the window to look at the peacock. Now she really had some exciting news to tell Eddie Wilson. This was hot news for sure!

Before Anna Patricia left for school she took a last look at the peacock. There it stood on the roof. As she walked up the street the peacock let out another screech. She could still hear it screeching while she waited for the school bus.

When the bus arrived, Anna Patricia climbed

aboard. She sat down beside Dumpty Peterson. "There's a peacock on the kitchen roof of the house next door to ours," she said.

"What's it doing there?" asked Dumpty.

"Just standing and making horrible screeches," said Anna Patricia. "We don't know where it came from, and I don't know how Mr. Smith will ever get it down. Isn't it exciting?"

"Bet it won't be there when you get home this afternoon," said Dumpty.

When Anna Patricia reached school she went straight to find Eddie. As soon as she saw him, she cried out, "Eddie! I've got some real exciting news! Guess what!"

"What?" said Eddie.

"There's a peacock on the roof next door to our house," said Anna Patricia.

"A peacock!" said Eddie. "A real one?"

"It's real all right," said Anna Patricia. "You should hear it."

"I never saw a real live peacock," said Eddie. "Do you think it will stay there until you get home from school?"

"Now we have some real exciting news for the paper," said Anna Patricia.

"You bet!" said Eddie. "Call me up if it's still there when you get home."

When Anna Patricia got home the peacock was still there. It was almost driving Mrs. Smith and Anna Patricia's mother crazy with its screeching. The longer the peacock stayed on the roof, the more it screeched.

Anna Patricia telephoned Eddie and he came over on his bicycle. He stood looking at the peacock with his mouth open. Then he said, "Annie Pat, this is wonderful! Now we have some real hot news and we

can have a 'Lost and Found' ad, too. You know! We'll
say: 'Found—a peacock.' And we'll put your telephone
number. Maybe we'll get a reward."

"We?" said Anna Patricia. "What do you mean, *we?*
I found it. I found it when I looked out of the window this morning."

"Okay! Okay!" said Eddie. "Maybe *you'll* get a reward."

"Oh, Eddie, I hope it stays until after the paper
comes out," said Anna Patricia.

"It has to stay, Annie Pat!" said Eddie. "It just has
to stay."

"But if it gets hungry it may fly away," said Anna
Patricia.

"That's right," said Eddie. He thought a moment
and then he said, "We have to feed it. If we feed it,
it won't fly away."

"What shall we feed it?" Anna Patricia asked.

"Corn, I guess," replied Eddie.

"Where will we get the corn?" inquired Anna Patricia.

"I know where I can buy a big bag of popcorn for ten cents," said Eddie. "I'll go get it."

"Do you think it will like popcorn?" said Anna Patricia.

"Sure it will like popcorn," said Eddie. "Everybody likes popcorn! I'll be right back."

Eddie rode off. Ten minutes later he was back with a big bag of popcorn. The children ran upstairs to Anna Patricia's room. Soon they were both leaning out the window, throwing popcorn onto the roof of the Smiths' kitchen. At first the peacock screeched louder than ever, but soon it quieted down and began to eat the popcorn.

"Annie Pat," said Eddie, when it was time for him to leave, "don't let it get away. Keep feeding it. I'll be back in the morning and we'll print the paper. But don't let it get away. We have to get the reward."

"Not *we,* Eddie," Anna Patricia called after him. "Me! I! Well, anyway not you."

CHAPTER 6

HOW TO CATCH A PEACOCK

IT WAS just daybreak when the peacock let out a screech that wakened Anna Patricia. She jumped out of bed and ran to the window sill. She took a handful of popcorn out of the bag and began throwing it, one piece at a time, onto the Smiths' roof. The peacock quieted down, but then Anna Patricia heard Mr. Smith's voice through the open window next door.

"I'm going to call the police!" she heard him say. "We have to get rid of that bird."

Oh, dear! thought Anna Patricia. If the police come to take it away, there won't be any "Lost and Found" in our paper.

Then she heard Mrs. Smith's voice. "Don't call them now. If the police come, they'll wake the whole neighborhood. Wait until after breakfast."

"Well, one more squawk out of that bird and I'm going to call the cops."

Anna Patricia decided that she would have to keep the peacock quiet, so she sat down on the window sill and watched it. Every time it showed any sign that it was about to screech, Anna Patricia threw it a piece of popcorn. She reached for a book and began to read. She sat on the window sill a long time. It was very quiet. Everyone had gone back to sleep except Anna Patricia.

After a while she heard her mother go downstairs. Then she heard Mr. Smith's voice again from next door. "Now I must do something about that peacock." Then she heard Mrs. Smith. "Oh," she said, "I'm sure it will go away. Please don't cause a lot of excitement."

Suddenly the peacock shrieked. The shriek was followed by a scream from Mr. Smith. "I can't stand that noise any longer. I'm going to call the police right now."

Anna Patricia jumped off the window sill and dashed downstairs. She ran to the telephone and dialed Eddie's number. Mr. Wilson answered. "Please may I speak to Eddie?" said Anna Patricia.

"I'll see if he's awake," said his father.

"It's terribly important," said Anna Patricia.

In a few moments Anna Patricia heard a very sleepy voice say, "Hello."

"Eddie!" said Anna Patricia. "Mr. Smith is calling the police to come take the peacock away."

Eddie woke up in a hurry. "What!" he yelled. "He can't do that to us. It's our peacock. It's our valuable property. We found it."

"What!" said Anna Patricia.

"I mean *you* found it. It has to be in our paper. We have to get the reward."

"What!" said Anna Patricia.

"I mean *you* have to get the reward," said Eddie. "I'll be right over."

Eddie rushed into the kitchen. "Have to get over to Annie Pat's right away, Mama. Got peacock trouble."

"Well, eat your breakfast first," said his mother. "Then you can go."

Eddie had already finished his orange juice and was pouring milk on his cereal. "This is enough, Mama," he said. "No eggs."

When Eddie rode up to Anna Patricia's on his bicycle, he could see a red police car parked in front of the Smiths' house. Behind the house he found Anna Patricia, all the boys and girls of the neighborhood, Mr. and Mrs. Smith, and in the midst of the crowd, Mr. Kilpatrick, the policeman. All the children knew Mr. Kilpatrick. On school days it was Mr. Kilpatrick who took the children across the big, wide street near the school. He was a special friend of Eddie's.

"Hello, Mr. Kilpatrick," said Eddie.

"Hello, Eddie," replied Mr. Kilpatrick. "I didn't think you would miss this show."

"I guess not!" said Eddie. "This is hot news."

"I think the way to get this bird down is to put some corn on the ground and not on the roof," said Mr. Kilpatrick. "Then it will come down when it gets hungry."

"What shall we do with it when it comes down?"

said Anna Patricia. "We have to keep it until we find out who owns it."

"We can put it in the garage," said Eddie.

"Not in my garage," said Mr. Smith. "I don't care who owns it. I tell you I'm tired of having that bird around."

"We'll put it in our garage," said Anna Patricia.

Anna Patricia's mother spoke up. "Anna Patricia, there's already enough in our garage without adding a peacock to it."

"Oh, Mummie!" pleaded Anna Patricia. "Just until we find out who owns it. Think how bad the person must feel who lost it! It's such a beautiful peacock."

"Very well," said Mrs. Wallace. "I hope the owner turns up soon."

Just then Boodles rode up on his bicycle. "I thought peacocks had big tails that stood up like a fan," he said. "This bird's tail just hangs down. I don't think it's a peacock."

"Yes, it is," said Mr. Kilpatrick. "They only spread their tails when they're on the ground, walking around and showing off. Very vain birds, peacocks. Like to show off."

"I wish this one would show off," said Boodles.

"Well now, we have to get some corn," said Mr. Kilpatrick.

"The popcorn is all gone," said Anna Patricia.

"I'll go get some corn," said Mr. Smith. "Anything to get this bird off my roof."

Mr. Smith backed his car out of the garage and drove off. Mrs. Smith and Mrs. Wallace went back into their kitchens, and Mr. Kilpatrick and the crowd of boys and girls sat down on the Smiths' porch and waited.

Eddie went into the Wallaces' garage and began to

set the type for the first copy of his newspaper. He had just got the heading *Hot News* set when he heard a commotion outside. Mr. Smith had returned with the corn. This time it was real chicken corn, not popcorn.

Eddie and Anna Patricia and all the children gathered around to watch Mr. Smith spread the corn on the ground around the kitchen.

"I could have done this without sending for the police," said Mr. Smith. "I thought you would get this pest off my roof, Officer."

"Sure, that's what I'm about," said Mr. Kilpatrick. "But you'll have to have a little patience. If you wanted somebody to catch it in a net, you should have sent for the dogcatcher. I notice that you didn't think of putting corn on the ground all day yesterday."

"Well, I hope it comes down to eat soon," said Mr. Smith.

"It will never come down as long as there's a crowd around—never! Now you children get out of here. Go back behind the house."

"Oh, Mr. Kilpatrick!" cried the children.

"Well then," said Mr. Kilpatrick, "hide yourselves and be quiet."

"Can we sit in your car?" asked Boodles.

"Sure, go sit in the car," said Mr. Kilpatrick. "But if you make any noise, I tell you right now I'm sending you home."

"Okay!" said the children, and they ran to the red car. After much pushing and shoving and a few shouts of "I want to sit there," they settled themselves—some inside and the rest all over the outside of Mr. Kilpatrick's car.

Mr. Kilpatrick sat down on the Smiths' porch, and Eddie went back to his printing job. He set another line of type. It said: "Peacock surprises Mr. and Mrs.

Smith. Anna Patricia Wallace finds peacock on their roof."

Every once in a while one of the children would get out of Mr. Kilpatrick's car, tiptoe up the Smiths' driveway, and peek around the corner to see if the peacock had come down. Then Mr. Kilpatrick would tiptoe around too and grab the peeker by the collar and march him (or her) back to the red car.

Every few minutes Eddie would take a look through the window in the Wallaces' garage, and so it was Eddie who saw the peacock come down off the roof and begin pecking at the corn. He rushed out the door. "It's down! It's down!" he yelled.

Anna Patricia and the rest of the children rushed from the car, and Mr. Kilpatrick came running from the porch. But the peacock was so frightened by all the commotion that it flew right back to the kitchen roof.

"Now you see what happened with all your racket?" said Mr. Kilpatrick. "We'll never catch this bird as long as this crowd is around here. You have to go home, all of you." Mr. Kilpatrick looked at his watch. "It's twelve o'clock," he said. "Time all of you went home for your lunch."

One by one the children departed. Eddie went back to the printing press, and Anna Patricia went into the house. Soon she came out with a tray loaded with peanut-butter sandwiches and three glasses of milk. "Mr. Kilpatrick," she said, "you come have lunch with Eddie and me in the garage."

"Thanks!" said Mr. Kilpatrick. "I will indeed. I can sit by the window and keep an eye on that bird. Ought to come down any minute now."

"Mr. Kilpatrick," said Eddie, munching a sandwich, "maybe if we called the fire department they would come and get the peacock down."

"The fire department!" exclaimed Mr. Kilpatrick. "Sure, and what can the fire department do that the police department can't do?"

"Oh, Eddie just likes to see the fire engines come," said Anna Patricia.

"I just thought maybe they would know how to get it down, that's all," said Eddie.

"Eddie, I'm surprised at you!" said Mr. Kilpatrick. "I always thought you admired the police force. I'm real disappointed."

"Oh, I do, Mr. Kilpatrick," said Eddie. "I think you're wonderful. I was just afraid the peacock might fly away and then we wouldn't get a reward."

"What?" said Anna Patricia.

"Oh, I mean *you* wouldn't get a reward," said Eddie.

Mr. Kilpatrick looked out the window. "Now what?" he cried.

The children ran to the window. "What?" said Anna Patricia.

"It's gone!" cried Mr. Kilpatrick. "It's nowhere in sight."

"Oh, I've lost the reward!" cried Anna Patricia.

The three of them rushed out of the door and around to the side of the Smiths' house. There was no peacock. They ran out front. There in the middle of the street was the peacock, with its beautiful tail raised like a big fan behind its head.

The children stood still in amazement. "Oh, dear!" cried Anna Patricia. "I'm afraid it will get run over by a car."

Mr. Kilpatrick did not seem to know just what to do, so he began to call, "Here, chick, chick, chick! Here, chick, chick, chick!"

The peacock lowered its tail and started to walk up the street, with its long train sweeping behind it.

119

Eddie ran and got the bag of corn off the porch. "Here, chick, chick, chick," he called, throwing corn toward the peacock. But still the peacock went on its way.

Then Mr. Kilpatrick had an idea. He ran back to the Wallaces' garage. When he came out he was carrying a large piece of a broken mirror. He tiptoed toward the peacock and finally got right in front of it. Eddie and Anna Patricia could not understand what Mr. Kilpatrick was trying to do. They were even more surprised when they saw him hold the mirror in front of the peacock.

What a funny thing to do! thought Eddie. Why is Mr. Kilpatrick letting the peacock see itself in the mirror?

But Mr. Kilpatrick knew. He knew that the peacock would think that it was seeing another peacock.

Sure enough! The peacock looked at itself and it

seemed pleased with what it saw. Mr. Kilpatrick began to turn around. The peacock turned around too. Mr. Kilpatrick began to walk backward, still holding the mirror. The peacock followed.

Eddie and Anna Patricia stood watching, with their mouths wide open. They watched Mr. Kilpatrick back up the driveway, with the peacock following. They watched him back into the garage. Then Eddie ran up the driveway behind the peacock, and when the bird was inside the garage, Eddie ducked inside too and closed the door. At last the peacock was safely shut in.

"Let me in," cried Anna Patricia. "Let me in!"

Eddie opened the door a crack, and Anna Patricia squeezed in.

"Now," said Mr. Kilpatrick, "here's the peacock. My work is finished for the day. It's up to you to find the owner."

As Mr. Kilpatrick squeezed himself out of the door, he said, "And now, I guess, you won't be thinking that the fire department is better than the police force!"

"You're wonderful, Mr. Kilpatrick!" Eddie cried.

"Yes, you are, Mr. Kilpatrick," said Anna Patricia.

Eddie went back to printing the paper. He added: "Police force is wonderful! Mr. Kilpatrick rescues peacock with mirror. Big mystery where it came from. To be continued next week." At the bottom of the sheet Eddie printed: "Lost and Found Department. Found—one peacock. Owner can get it by telephoning West 5-7382."

Anna Patricia read it through. Then she said, "Eddie! You didn't say, 'Reward.' They always say, 'Reward.'"

"But you only say, 'Reward' when you lose something," said Eddie, "and you want to get it back. Then you say, 'Reward.'"

"But they did lose something," said Anna Patricia. "They lost their peacock, didn't they?"

Eddie sat down on a soapbox. "Annie Pat," he said, "sometimes you get me all mixed up."

CHAPTER 7

THE REWARD

WHEN all the copies of *Hot News* were printed, Eddie and Anna Patricia rushed off to distribute them. Then Anna Patricia hurried home to wait for the telephone call from the owner of the peacock.

When she came into the house, her father said, "I've just read the first copy of *Hot News*."

126

"Oh, Daddy, did you like it?" said Anna Patricia. "Did you see the Lost and Found Department?"

"Yes, I did," said her father. "Don't be disappointed, Anna Patricia, if you don't hear from the owner, because the owner of that bird does not live in this neighborhood or in Eddie Wilson's neighborhood. I'm sure that bird flew in from the country."

"How do you know?" asked Anna Patricia.

"Because if anyone owned peacocks in this neighborhood, or in Eddie's, we would all know about it."

"Oh, Daddy!" said Anna Patricia, in a very sad voice. She sat thinking. Then her face brightened. "Well, Daddy," she said, "if we don't hear from the person who owns it, why then, 'finders, keepers'! The peacock will be mine!"

"Anna Patricia!" said her father. "You cannot keep the peacock. There is no place here to keep a peacock."

"But what will we do with the poor peacock," said

Anna Patricia, "if we can't find out who owns it?"

"Send it to a zoo," said her father.

The following morning, at about nine o'clock, the telephone rang. Dr. Wallace answered it. "Is this West 5-7382?" asked a woman's voice.

"Yes, it is," replied Dr. Wallace.

"Are you the people who have the peacock?" the voice then asked.

Dr. Wallace almost jumped with surprise. "Yes," he said, "we have the peacock."

"I am Mrs. Strong," said the voice at the other end of the telephone. "The peacock flew away from my place, and I should like very much to get it back. It's one of the finest birds I have. It has the most beautiful train of the lot. You see, I raise peacocks."

"You do?" said Dr. Wallace. "Why do you raise peacocks? Don't they drive you crazy with their noise? By the way, I am Dr. Wallace."

128

"Oh, no, Dr. Wallace!" replied Mrs. Strong. "You get used to their voices."

"Well," said Dr. Wallace, "I had never thought of a peacock as having a voice, but I guess the racket it makes does come from its voice."

Mrs. Strong laughed. "They're such friendly birds," she said, "unless they feel that you don't like them. You see, I live alone and I find them very good company."

"I see," said Dr. Wallace. "Now how can we get this bird back to you? Where do you live?"

Mrs. Strong told Dr. Wallace where she lived and how to reach her house.

"I'll be glad to bring the peacock back to you this afternoon," said Dr. Wallace. "But tell me, what's the best way to fix up a peacock for traveling? Never having taken even a short trip with a peacock, I don't know much about it."

"Well, the best way is to put it in a wooden box," said Mrs. Strong, "and nail a few sticks across the top."

"But how do I put it in the box?" asked Dr. Wallace.

"Oh, just pick it up," said Mrs. Strong. "It's all very simple."

"Well, I'll do my best," said Dr. Wallace. "By the way, how did you happen to find out that we had your peacock?"

"Oh," replied Mrs. Strong, "a friend of mine telephoned and asked me if I had lost a peacock. She said she saw a piece about it in a newspaper that a little boy in her neighborhood is printing, and she thought of me."

"You don't say!" exclaimed Dr. Wallace. "I never would have believed it possible."

Meanwhile, Anna Patricia had been standing by

her father's elbow. She was so excited that she could hardly keep still. When her father hung up, Anna Patricia said, "Did she say anything about the reward?"

"Not a word," replied her father.

"She'll probably think of it when we take the peacock back," said Anna Patricia.

When Anna Patricia telephoned the news to Eddie, he was very excited. "When are you going to take it back?" he asked.

"This afternoon," replied Anna Patricia, "and you can go with us. Come over to my house right after dinner."

As soon as dinner was over, Dr. Wallace went to the basement to see if he could find a wooden box for the peacock. He looked around, but he did not see anything large enough. "I'll have to see if Mr. Smith has a box," he said.

When he asked him, Mr. Smith said, "If I haven't

one I'll build one. Anything to help that peacock get on its way home. I'm going to put a sign on my roof, *No Parking for Peacocks!*"

Mr. Smith had just brought a box into the Wallaces' garage when Eddie rode up on his bicycle.

"We're going to put the peacock in a box," Anna Patricia shouted to Eddie.

"Now keep the door shut," said Dr. Wallace. "We don't want this bird to escape." Eddie closed the door.

The car was outside, and the peacock stood in the center of the empty garage. It looked steadily at Mr. Smith, and it did not look pleased with Mr. Smith. Mr. Smith turned his back on the peacock to make certain that the door was closed tightly. As soon as his back was turned, the peacock dashed up to him, nipped him on the leg, and gave him a whack on the legs with its wing. Then the peacock darted off to the other side of the garage.

"Ouch!" cried Mr. Smith. "He nipped me! That good-for-nothing peacock bit me!"

"That's because he knows you don't like him," said Dr. Wallace.

"Is that so!" said Mr. Smith. "Well, do you like him?"

"Oh, my, yes!" said Dr. Wallace, stepping carefully toward the bird to pick it up. "Nice peacock!"

The peacock ran. Then the peacock and Dr. Wallace both began running around the garage, and soon it was hard to tell whether Dr. Wallace was chasing the peacock or whether the peacock was chasing Dr. Wallace. Dr. Wallace was not sure either, but he kept running. "See if you can drive it into a corner," he called out.

Eddie and Anna Patricia joined in the chase. Mr. Smith kept out of the way.

"That's good," said Dr. Wallace. "Now we have

him." Dr. Wallace reached out, picked up the bird, and placed it in the wooden box. As he did so, there was a cry of "Oh! Oh!" from both the children and a shout from Mr. Smith.

"Look!" cried Eddie, pointing to the place on the floor where the peacock had stood. Dr. Wallace looked and there, lying on the floor, was the whole train of the peacock. All its beautiful feathers lay spread out on the floor.

"Oh, Daddy!" cried Anna Patricia. "Look what you did!"

Dr. Wallace looked in the box at the peacock. He could not believe that it didn't have its tail. But it didn't. Not a single tail feather was left. "But I couldn't have done that!" he said. "I picked it up gently."

Anna Patricia picked up the beautiful feathers. "Oh, what will the lady say!" she exclaimed.

Eddie examined them. "They're pretty. I'll bet the lady will be awful mad."

Dr. Wallace began nailing some slats across the top of the box. The peacock's head and neck stuck up through the slats.

"Don't turn your back on it," said Mr. Smith. "It has a mean look in its eye."

Eddie and Anna Patricia were busy examining the feathers. Anna Patricia thought the colors were beautiful. She waved them back and forth. The shades of blue and green shimmered with a dark bronze color. "Look as though they'd been painted, don't they?" said Anna Patricia.

"Sure do," said Eddie, who was already getting ideas as to what could be done with the feathers. "You know what?" he said. "These are real valuable property. A fellow could trade a whole lot of swell stuff for these feathers."

"That's right, Eddie," said Anna Patricia. "Maybe somebody would trade me a doll for some of them."

Then her father spoke up. "Those tail feathers belong to the woman who owns this bird," he said.

"You mean, Daddy, that we have to take them back to her?"

"I do," said her father firmly. "They are part of her bird."

The children looked sad. They were to have no peacock and no feathers.

By this time the peacock was safely in the box. "Come along now," said Dr. Wallace. "Let's get going." He looked at Mr. Smith. "Want to come along?" he asked.

"No, thanks!" said Mr. Smith. "I shall be delighted to stand by the curb and wave good-by to that peacock. May I never see another!"

"Same here!" said Dr. Wallace. "But I wouldn't

138

want the old bird to hear me." He picked up the box and started for the car. Anna Patricia followed her father. She was carrying the bunch of feathers. Eddie brought up the rear.

The box was too big to go on the floor of the car, so Dr. Wallace had to put it on the back seat. As Anna Patricia climbed in beside the box, she said, "Oh, look! The peacock can look out the window."

"Oh, yes!" cried Eddie. "See, Dr. Wallace, the peacock's looking out the window."

"That's just dandy!" said Dr. Wallace. "I hope it doesn't start talking about what it sees, because I don't like that bird's voice."

He started the car and soon they were outside the town, rolling along past fields and farmhouses. After a while they entered the main street of another town. Here Dr. Wallace drove more slowly. There were a lot of cars on the street, and the pavements were full of people out for a Sunday-afternoon walk. Just as Dr. Wallace's car reached the center of town, *pop!* went a tire on one of the back wheels. *Bump, bump, bump!* went the wheel.

"I think you have a flat," Eddie called out.

Dr. Wallace drove over to the curb and stopped the car. He got out and walked around to the back of the car. Sure enough! He had a flat tire. It was as flat as a pancake. He opened the trunk of the car and took out the jack.

Eddie and Anna Patricia jumped out. "Have to change the tire, don't you?" said Eddie.

"Yes, I do," said Dr. Wallace. "You can help. You can hold the nuts."

"Okay!" said Eddie.

Anna Patricia stood by. The peacock gawked out the window. Soon passers-by noticed the peacock. "Oh, look at that bird!" people called out. Before long a crowd gathered. Then people driving cars noticed the crowd. Cars began to stop. Cars began parking all along both sides of the street. Soon people could not walk on the pavement at all, the crowd was so big. Those nearest the car asked questions about the peacock, and Eddie and Anna Patricia were delighted to tell the whole story. Of course, the people on the outer edge of the crowd could not see anything. Some of them began to ask, "What's the matter? Accident?" Others replied, "Guess so. Can't see."

"Anybody hurt?"

"Don't know."

"Has anybody sent for an ambulance?"

A man who had just joined the crowd said, "I'm a doctor."

Somebody else said, "Here's a doctor. Let the doctor through."

Everyone began saying, "Let the doctor through."

The people stood aside, and the doctor made his way to the car.

"Stand aside. Stand aside, please," he said. "Where is the injured party?"

A woman turned to him and said, "Isn't that the cutest thing? Just look at that peacock! I declare it looks human."

"Is this all it is?" said the doctor in surprise.

"We have a flat tire," said Anna Patricia.

The doctor muttered to himself and moved out of the crowd.

Just then a siren sounded. It was the police. Two police cars drove up and six policemen got out. "Break it up!" they called out. "Move along. You're obstructing traffic."

People began getting back into their cars. "I think it's terrible," said one woman. "That ambulance isn't here yet. The poor soul!"

Prodded by the police, the crowd began to move away. Finally the six policemen reached the car. Dr. Wallace was just fastening the last nut.

"What's going on here?" said one policeman.

"Flat tire," replied Dr. Wallace.

"Don't give me any funny talk," said the policeman, "or I'll take you straight to the police station. A crowd like that doesn't gather to watch a man change a tire. What are you up to?"

"It was the peacock," said Anna Patricia. "They were all looking at the peacock."

"Peacock!" said the policeman.

"Yes! See!" said Anna Patricia, pointing to the window of the car.

"Well, what do you know about that!" said one of the policemen. "Looks almost human."

"Does, at that," said another policeman.

Dr. Wallace got back into his car. Before he drove

away, the six policemen lined up on each side of the car and looked at the peacock. The peacock stared back at them. Then it nodded its head like royalty.

It was almost dark when the car drove up to Mrs. Strong's old white farmhouse. Dr. Wallace carefully lifted the box out of the car and carried it up to the front door.

"Here, Eddie," said Anna Patricia, "you can carry its tail."

"I don't want to carry it," said Eddie. "You carry it, Annie Pat. You found the peacock. You carry the tail."

"Maybe we better just leave it here on the seat," said Anna Patricia. "Maybe the lady won't notice that the peacock doesn't have its tail." Anna Patricia laid the feathers on the seat, and the two children ran after Dr. Wallace.

When Mrs. Strong opened the door, she said, "Oh,

you've brought the peacock! I'm so glad to get Professor back. I call this one Professor. He looks so wise. He really is my best bird."

Dr. Wallace cleared his throat. "I'm sorry to tell you we had an accident," he said.

"An accident!" said Mrs. Strong. "What happened?"

Dr. Wallace turned to Anna Patricia. "Anna Patricia," he said, "where is the tail?"

Anna Patricia looked around as though she expected to find it lying on the floor. Then she said, "Oh, Eddie, you go get it out of the car."

Eddie went off to get the peacock feathers. He was going to have to carry them after all.

"Oh," said Mrs. Strong, "don't worry about it. Sometimes, when they get frightened, peacocks just shed their trains. But they soon grow them back again."

"You mean I didn't pull its tail feathers out?" said Dr. Wallace.

"No," replied Mrs. Strong. "I suppose it was frightened when you tried to put it in the box."

By this time Eddie was back with the feathers. "This is Eddie, Mrs. Strong," said Dr. Wallace, "and this is my daughter, Anna Patricia."

"Now, Eddie," said Mrs. Strong, "if you would like to have those feathers, you may keep them."

"Oh, thanks!" said Eddie. "I sure would. Thank you very much."

Eddie looked at Anna Patricia, and he thought he had never seen her look so surprised.

"Now," said Mrs. Strong, "I know you're hungry. Come and have some cake and cocoa."

Dr. Wallace and the children sat down at the table in the dining room and ate coconut cake and drank cups of cocoa, while Mrs. Strong told them all about

peacocks. She told them that she had started out with two and that now she had twenty-seven. By the time she stopped talking, Dr. Wallace was not only full of coconut cake and cocoa, he was also fed up with peacocks.

When they got up to leave, Mrs. Strong said, "Now just wait a minute. I want to give these children a reward, because if it hadn't been for them I wouldn't have got my lovely peacock back."

"I found it," said Anna Patricia.

"But I printed the paper," said Eddie, as Mrs. Strong left the room.

She was gone a long time. Anna Patricia kept looking at the feathers, which Eddie held in his hand like a big plume.

When Mrs. Strong returned she was carrying two cardboard cartons. "Now," she said, "I want you each to have one of these." She held the cartons out to the children. They looked inside. What did they see? *Peacocks!*

"Baby ones," said Mrs. Strong.

Dr. Wallace sat down on the nearest chair. He felt dizzy. He thought he saw twenty-seven peacocks.

Eddie handed over half of the feathers to Anna Patricia and picked up his peacock.

CHAPTER 8

EDDIE FINDS A DOLL

EDDIE spent every spare minute in the Wallaces'
garage with the printing press. One Saturday
evening, after Eddie had printed his weekly edition
of *Hot News* and gone home, Anna Patricia's father
said to her, "Anna Patricia, why don't you give that
printing press to Eddie? You never use it, and Eddie

is crazy about it. He knows what to do with a printing press."

"No," said Anna Patricia, "I won't give that printing press to Eddie. It's my only treasure. Eddie gets everything. You made me put my little peacock out on the Wilsons' farm with Eddie's. It was just like giving him my peacock. Now you want me to give him my printing press."

"All right! All right!" said her father. "Soon we'll have to put a bed in our garage for Eddie. He only goes home to sleep. Suppose you had to go over to Eddie's house every time you wanted to play with your dolls!"

"I don't have very many dolls," said Anna Patricia, "and I like my printing press."

The following week was a very important week to Eddie. It was the town's annual Clean-up Week. This was the week when everyone gathered together the things they no longer wanted, which were then sold to help swell the Community Chest fund. The sale was always held in a big empty store on Main Street. Each year Eddie went to the sale with the money he had saved. He had got lots of his valuable property in this way.

On Monday afternoon, on his way home from school, Eddie stopped in at the store. There were piles of things heaped on the floor, and several women were sorting them over. Eddie looked around. The store was fairyland to Eddie. And then one of the women said, "Run along, little boy. The sale is tomorrow. Run along now. You're in the way."

Eddie moved toward the door. Just before he went out he passed a pile of broken toys. Sitting on top of the lot was an old doll. She was a big doll, and she looked as though someone had treated her quite badly. She had lost her wig, and a big hole showed in the top of her head. But even through the dirt on her face Eddie could see that she was pretty. She was wearing a faded, mussed-up blue dress and, in spite of her battered state, she made Eddie think of Anna Patricia. Suddenly he had an idea. He ran back to the woman who had spoken to him and said, "Couldn't I just buy that doll over there? Couldn't I?"

The woman stopped her work and looked over to where Eddie was pointing. "Well, now," she said, "aren't you a sweet brother to think of a doll for your sister!" She turned to her helpers. "Shall we let this little boy have that doll?"

"Oh, yes, let him have it," said the others.

"How much is it?" Eddie asked.

"I guess ten cents is about right," said the woman. Eddie dug into his pocket and pulled out ten cents. "Take it along," said the woman.

"Well . . . well, could you wrap it up?" said Eddie.

154

"Oh, no!" she replied. "We haven't any wrapping paper yet."

"Okay," said Eddie, but he had a worried frown on his face as he picked up the big doll. Before he left he peeked out the door. He looked up and down the street. There was no one in sight, so he went outside. He decided to keep to the back way, so he dashed around the corner and ducked into a narrow street. Right away he knew that he had made a mistake, for there were two boys playing ball in the street. Eddie ran back quickly to Main Street. There he found three boys coming toward him. Eddie put the doll on a step in a doorway and walked on. When the three boys passed him, Eddie was looking in a store window. He made believe that he was very much interested in something in the window. He made believe so well that he did not see a big Dalmatian dog come around the corner. The dog went right up to the doll, and in a moment he had taken it in his mouth and was running away with it.

When the boys were out of sight, Eddie went back for the doll. He was surprised to find that it was gone. Then he thought perhaps he had forgotten where he had left it, so he looked in other doorways. When he failed to find the doll he went on his way, feeling very puzzled.

He had gone about two blocks when he saw, lying on the sidewalk of the next block, something that looked like the doll. He began to run. When he had gone about half the distance, he saw a man stoop down and pick up the doll. The man looked at the doll. Then he looked around. Eddie saw him put the doll in a baby carriage that was parked on the sidewalk. The man walked on.

When Eddie reached the baby carriage, he found that it was standing right beside the door of a grocery

store. A baby was sitting in the carriage and had just taken a firm clutch on the doll's dress. Eddie reached in and took hold of the doll. The baby screamed. Eddie tugged. The baby screamed louder. The door of the grocery store opened and out came a woman with a big bundle in her arms. She looked at Eddie and the baby and said to Eddie, "Aren't you ashamed of yourself! A great big boy like you, tormenting that little baby! Take your hands off that doll."

"But it's mine," said Eddie.

"Oh, so it's yours!" said the woman with the bundle. "So you play with dolls, do you?" She went on her way.

Just then the door opened again and another woman came out. She looked at the doll in the carriage and her eyes grew very big. She grabbed the doll away from the baby and looked at Eddie. "What do you mean by putting that filthy dirty doll in my baby's carriage?" she shouted. She pushed the doll into Eddie's arms and angrily wheeled the screaming baby away.

Eddie stood holding the doll. If only I could get a paper bag! he thought. He looked through the door of the grocery store. There were several people inside, but he just had to have a paper bag. Eddie held the doll behind his back and went in. "What do you want, son?" said a man who was leaning over a basket of potatoes.

"Would you please give me a paper bag?" said Eddie.

Without looking up, the man reached into a shelf under the counter and handed Eddie a paper bag. It would only have held the doll's head.

"I have to have a bigger one," said Eddie.

"Well, help yourself," said the man. "I'm busy."

Eddie backed into a basket of apples and dropped

the doll on top of the apples. Then he stooped down and began looking through the paper bags. There were many sizes, but none large enough. Wherever, thought Eddie frantically, are the big ones?

He was still shuffling through the paper bags when he heard a man's voice say, "Who left this doll baby in the apple basket?" Eddie looked around, and there stood one of the clerks with the doll in his hand. He was holding it up, and everyone in the store had turned to look at him.

Eddie could feel his face burning. He went on looking for a paper bag. Then he heard the man's voice again. "Somebody is always leaving something around here. Doll babies in the apples! Yesterday it was a wooden soldier in the onions." Then he called out, "Bill, if anybody comes back for this, it's right up here."

Just then Eddie came upon a big paper bag. He

straightened up and looked around. There sat the doll on the very top shelf, between the corn flakes and the saltine crackers.

"Did you get your bag, son?" said the first man.

"Yes, I found one," said Eddie. "Thanks."

"Well, so long!" said the man.

Eddie lingered. In a few minutes the man said, "What else do you want?"

Eddie looked along the shelves. "I . . . I . . . I'm just looking," he said.

"Can't you remember what your mother told you to get?" said the man.

Eddie gulped. "Uh," he said. "Uh—have you any pickles?"

"Sure!" said the man. "How many do you want?"

"Just one," said Eddie.

The grocery man put a pickle in a bag and handed it to Eddie. "A nickel," he said.

Eddie handed over a nickel and went outside. He stood on the sidewalk by the door and ate the pickle. He watched the customers go in and out the door. The store was not empty for a single moment. He had almost finished the pickle when he noticed that there was no one in the store. Eddie darted in. "You back again?" said the grocer. "Forget something?"

At that moment the door opened, and in came two big boys who were friends of Eddie's brother Rudy. "Hi, Eddie!" they shouted.

The grocer was looking down at Eddie. "Hurry up, son. What do you want?" he said.

Eddie hesitated. Then he said, "Uh—have you got any cinnamon buns?"

"No cinnamon buns," said the man.

"Well . . . uh . . . I guess I'll take an apple," said Eddie.

The man picked an apple out of the basket and

handed it to Eddie. "Three cents," he said. Eddie handed over three cents and left the store. Again he stood outside. He munched the apple. He hoped he was not going to have to spend any more of his money. First the doll, then the pickle, and now the apple. He had spent almost a quarter.

In and out, in and out the door went the customers. At last the store was empty again. Eddie tore in like a ball of fire. "Please, mister!" he cried, pointing up at the doll. "That's mine. Can I have it quick, mister?"

The grocer looked very surprised, but he reached up and lifted the doll down. He laughed as he handed it to Eddie. Then he said, "Why didn't you say so before?"

Eddie stuffed the doll into the big paper bag. "I couldn't," he said. "I'm not going to keep it. It's for somebody else. I hate it."

Eddie had never been so glad to open his own front

door. He ran right down to the basement. Now he would see what could be done with this doll. He knew it would need a lot of fixing before he could offer it to Anna Patricia in exchange for the printing press. It would have to look pretty super. First thing, he thought, I have to see if I can get it clean.

He took the doll out of the paper bag and put it in the washtub. He poured some soap flakes in and turned on the water. The running water made so much noise that he did not hear Joe and Frank come down the basement stairs. They were at his elbow before he knew that they were there. The twins looked over Eddie's shoulder. When they saw the big doll sitting in the tub they both screamed. "Why, Eddie!" cried Joe. "Aren't you the cute little thing! Where did you get that sweet little dolly?"

"Eddie!" cried Frank. "What a dear little snookie-ookums!"

There was a piece of hose attached to the spigot. Eddie reached for the hose, turned on the water full force, put his finger across the end of the hose, and sprayed it in the direction of his brothers. The boys ran from the shower bath.

Mrs. Wilson came down to see what the racket was about.

"Mother!" cried Joe. "Your youngest son has a doll baby."

"Mama!" Eddie cried. "Please come help me. I don't know what to do with this thing."

Mrs. Wilson went over to Eddie. "Look, Mama," he said, "I'm going to trade this doll for Anna Patricia's printing press. If it looks nice I know she'll trade. Anna Patricia wants to collect dolls."

Mrs. Wilson picked up the dripping doll. "Well, Eddie," she said, "it will need a lot of fixing, I'm afraid, before Anna Patricia will look at it."

Eddie sat down on a nearby stool. "Do you think you can do it, Mama?" he said.

Mrs. Wilson looked at the doll. "It needs everything," she said. "First of all, it needs a wig."

Eddie's face lighted up. "Oh, I know where I can get a wig," he said. "Anyway, I think I can."

CHAPTER 9

WIG! WIG! WHO'S GOT THE WIG!

THAT evening Eddie went over to see Sidney. He was carrying his bunch of peacock feathers. Sidney was in her room feeding her fish. "Hi, Sid!" Eddie called out.

"I'm up here," Sidney called back. "Come on up." When Eddie came into the room, Sidney said, "I've got guppies."

Eddie was not interested in guppies. He had something else on his mind. He lost no time in bringing up the subject. "Sid," said Eddie, "you never wear that wig I gave you. Don't you like it?"

"Oh," replied Sidney, "my mother wouldn't let me wear it. She said it was just for Halloween."

"Well, Sid," said Eddie, "if you'll give me that wig, I'll give you these peacock feathers."

"Oh, I traded the wig for these guppies," said Sidney. "I traded with Dumpty Peterson. He wanted the wig for his Indian collection. He said it was a good scalp."

Eddie looked like a balloon without any air in it. "Oh!" he said. Down came the bunch of peacock feathers that he had been carrying like a bouquet. Now they dragged on the floor. He sat down with the bunch of feathers between his knees. "Sidney," he said, "I have to have that wig. It's important."

171

"Why?" Sidney asked him. "What do you want it for?"

"I want it for something special," said Eddie.

"Well, Dumpty has it," said Sidney. Then she said, "They're awfully pretty feathers, Eddie."

Eddie looked down at the feathers. Very slowly he pulled a long one from the bunch and said, "Do you want this one, Sid?"

"Oh, yes!" cried Sidney. "I'd love it!" Eddie handed it to Sidney. "Thanks!" she said.

"Welcome!" said Eddie. He was still looking very glum.

"Eddie," said Sidney, "I think you're very generous. You're always giving things away. You gave me that wig and now you gave me this peacock feather. Don't you ever trade, Eddie?"

"Well, I like to trade," said Eddie, "but it's so hard. Nobody ever wants to trade with me."

"I trade a lot," said Sidney. " 'Course I'm not allowed to trade without asking Mum first. Mum says I can always trade guppies, 'cause there are always more guppies. I have twice as many now as I had when Dumpty traded for the wig."

"You have?" said Eddie.

"If you'd like to have some," said Sidney, "I'll give you some. You don't have to trade. I'll give them to you."

"I would like some," said Eddie.

"Well, let's find a jar," said Sidney.

The children went down to the basement, where they found Sidney's father working with his jig saw. "Pappy," said Sidney, "have you got a jar? I'm going to give Eddie some guppies."

"Fine!" said Mr. Stewart. "Good idea! Here's a jar."

This was the first time Eddie had been in the Stewarts' basement since the day the family moved in. He looked around and was surprised to see in the center of the floor a brightly painted totem pole, which reached the ceiling.

"Remember the day we unpacked the station wagon?" said Sidney. Then she waved her hand toward a pile of cartons. "This is all my stuff," she said. "I haven't had time to unpack it."

Suddenly Eddie thought of something. "Say, Sid," he said, "what was it that you got that night right after you moved in here?"

Sidney pointed to the totem pole. "That!" she said. "My totem pole. My grandmother sent it to me from Alaska. The Indians make them. When Pappy and I went to the freight station to get it, the man said it was the only totem pole he had ever had in the station."

Eddie walked over to the totem pole. He touched it

and said, "That sure is swell." Up went the bunch of peacock feathers, which were still in his hand. He waved them back and forth as he admired the totem pole. "It sure is swell," he said.

"Of course, I'm not allowed to trade my totem pole," said Sidney.

Eddie let out a sigh. Down went the feathers.

When Eddie returned home, his mother said, "Did you get the wig?"

"No," replied Eddie, "but I got some guppies."

"Guppies!" exclaimed his mother. "What are you going to do with guppies?"

"Oh, they'll come in handy," said Eddie.

"I certainly hope you'll let them come in handy before they fill the bathtub," said his mother.

When Eddie reached school the following day, he went straight to Dumpty Peterson and said, "I've got some swell guppies. I'll trade with you."

"I have guppies," said Dumpty.

"How about some peacock feathers?" said Eddie. "You never saw more beautiful peacock feathers."

"I have some peacock feathers," Dumpty replied. "I traded with Anna Patricia. I gave her that wig that was Sidney's for the peacock feathers."

This news was a terrible blow to Eddie. Anna Patricia had the wig—the wig that he was counting on for the doll! Eddie had to take some time to think this over. He wondered what Anna Patricia wanted with the wig. She had not wanted it when he had offered it to her. Why did she want it now?

By the time school was out, Eddie had decided to try the guppies on Anna Patricia. As usual, he rode over to her house on his bicycle to do some printing. It was hard to carry a jar of guppies on his bicycle, but he reached Anna Patricia's without spilling them. He was busy setting type when Anna Patricia came into the garage. "Hello, Eddie!" she said. "What are you doing?"

"I'm printing some cards," replied Eddie.

"What kind of cards?" Anna Patricia asked.

"My business cards," replied Eddie.

Eddie handed a card to Anna Patricia. She read it. It said: "Edward Wilson. All kinds of printing done. Ask for prices. Cheap."

"That's nice," said Anna Patricia.

"Got any news for the paper yet?" Eddie asked.

"Mrs. Johnson has a new baby," said Anna Patricia.

"That's good," said Eddie. "Everybody always thinks new babies are hot news. I think it's silly, but you gotta please your customers."

Then Eddie looked up at Anna Patricia. "Annie Pat," he said, "have you got that wig that Sidney traded to Dumpty and Dumpty traded to you?"

"Oh, yes!" said Anna Patricia.

"Well, Annie Pat," said Eddie, "if you'll give me that wig, I'll give you some guppies."

"No, I want the wig," said Anna Patricia.

"But you didn't want it before when I offered it to you," said Eddie.

"If you wanted it," said Anna Patricia, "why did you give it to Sidney?"

" 'Cause you said Sidney wanted a wig," said Eddie.

"Well, you didn't have to give it to her just because I said that," said Anna Patricia. "If you wanted it, you should have kept it."

"What do you want it for?" Eddie asked.

"I think it will come in handy if I need to make some dolls' wigs sometime," said Anna Patricia.

Eddie could hardly believe his ears. "Oh, Annie Pat!" he said. "Wigs are awfully hard to make. You couldn't do that."

"Well, my mother could," Anna Patricia replied calmly.

Eddie was stuck. He decided to try again. "Won't you give it to me for the guppies?" he said. "They're awful nice guppies. They make more and more all the time."

"But I don't collect guppies," said Anna Patricia. "I collect dolls."

"Yeah, I know," said Eddie.

Eddie went home, feeling very unhappy. When he walked into the house he said, "Mama, Annie Pat has that wig and she won't let me have it. Not even for the guppies."

"Don't fret about it," said his mother. "We'll find a wig for the doll."

"Maybe Annie Pat won't trade me the printing press," said Eddie. "Maybe she won't trade it even for the doll."

hink if it is beautiful enough she will," replied his mother.

"It can't be beautiful without any hair," said Eddie.

"We'll get her fixed up," said his mother. "Just be patient."

"Will you fix her up so she will knock Annie Pat's eye out?" said Eddie.

His mother laughed. "You just trust me, Eddie," she replied.

Eddie felt much better.

The following day at school Anna Patricia said, "Eddie, what do you want with that wig?"

"I can't tell you," said Eddie. "It's a secret. But it's very important."

Anna Patricia pulled out a paper bag from inside her desk. "Here, Eddie," she said, "you can have the wig."

Eddie ran home from school as though he had wings on his feet. He rushed into the house, calling, "Mama! Mama!"

"I'm up here in the sewing room," his mother called down.

Eddie appeared in a moment at the sewing-room door. He held up the paper bag. "Got it!" he cried. "She gave it to me!"

"That's good," said his mother. "Now we can finish this doll."

Mrs. Wilson took the wig out of Eddie's hand and began to cut and shape a piece of it to fit the doll's head. Eddie went off to put some air in his bicycle tires.

When he returned, his mother called to him. "Eddie," she said, "come see if you think Anna Patricia will like this doll, now that it's finished."

Eddie went into the sewing room. He looked at the

doll. He could not believe it was the same doll that he had bought for ten cents. This doll looked like a fairy with golden curls. His mother had dressed it in some thin white stuff and had sewed something that looked like diamonds all over it. There was a blue velvet cape with a hood, and even little red shoes.

"Oh, Mama!" said Eddie. "I don't know much about dolls, but that sure looks super to me."

"I have a box that will hold her, too," said his mother.

"I'll take it over to Annie Pat's right now," said Eddie.

"I'll drive you over," said his mother. "You can't manage the box on your bicycle."

"Oh, that's swell of you, Mama," said Eddie.

It did not take long for Eddie and his mother to reach Anna Patricia's house. As Eddie got out of the car, Mrs. Wilson hoped that Anna Patricia had not

changed her mind about trading the printing press for a doll. She knew that Eddie would be heartbroken if she had.

"I'll wait here in the car for you, Eddie," said his mother.

"Okay!" said Eddie.

Mrs. Wilson watched him as he carried the big box very carefully up to Anna Patricia's front door. By this time she was just as anxious for Eddie to get the printing press as Eddie was.

Eddie rang the doorbell, and Anna Patricia opened the door. "Hello, Eddie!" she said. "What have you got?"

"Oh, Annie Pat! I have something for you," said Eddie. "Just wait till you see it!"

"For me?" said Anna Patricia.

Eddie put the box down and began to untie the string. "You remember, Annie Pat," he said, "you said if I ever found a doll for you, you'd give me the printing press?"

"Well," said Anna Patricia, sounding a little uncertain. "You know I said maybe. I didn't say for sure."

But then Eddie lifted the lid, and Anna Patricia had her first glimpse of the doll. "Oh!" she said. "Oh! She's beautiful!"

Eddie sighed with relief. "Do you like it, Annie Pat?"

"Oh, yes!" she replied. "You can have the printing press, Eddie."

"Yippee! Yippee!" yelled Eddie.

Anna Patricia's father opened the door of his office. "What is all this racket?" he asked.

"Annie Pat gave me the printing press!" Eddie shouted. "She gave me the printing press!"

"That's great!" said Dr. Wallace. "Come along. I

see your mother outside in the car. I'll help you put the printing press in the trunk of the car."

"Oh, thanks!" said Eddie.

Eddie and Dr. Wallace carried the printing press out of the garage and placed it very carefully in the trunk of the car.

Eddie was beaming as he rode home beside his mother. "Now I can print all I want, Mama," he said. "I can print my newspaper and cards and ads and all kinds of things. I can make money, Mama!" He looked up at his mother and grinned. "And do you know what, Mama?"

"What?" said his mother.

"I'm going to buy you a present," said Eddie. "Tell you what, Mama. I'll buy you a new hat."

"With peacock feathers in it, Eddie?" said his mother. And they both laughed very hard.

When they had almost reached home, Eddie said,

"You know, Mama, Annie Pat's a good egg." After a while he added, "And so is Sidney. I'm going to help her unpack all those boxes. Bet she has some swell stuff —real valuable property."

CAROLYN HAYWOOD's career as one of America's most popular authors of children's books began in 1939, with the publication of *"B" Is for Betsy*. Since then Miss Haywood has written sixteen books, to the delight of millions of children. As the *New York Herald Tribune* remarked, "She knows her small children inside out."

Miss Haywood was born in Philadelphia and now lives in Chestnut Hill, a suburb of that city. She is a graduate of the Philadelphia Normal School and studied at the Pennsylvania Academy of the Fine Arts, where she won the Cresson European Scholarship for distinguished work. Miss Haywood calls herself a "grand-pupil" of the great American illustrator, Howard Pyle, since she studied with three of his famous pupils, Elizabeth Shippen Green Elliott, Violet Oakley, and Jessie Willcox Smith. Her continuing experience in the painting of children's portraits has given her a sympathetic understanding of them and their interests and has made her peculiarly well fitted to write and illustrate for them. During the last year she has executed numerous commissions both in her own community and in other parts of the country. One of her paintings is part of the permanent collection at the Pennsylvania Academy of the Fine Arts in Philadelphia.